Melissa Witlow needs help, but Rachel is already caring for nine little children; how can she possibly make room for three more people . . . ?

When tears glistened on the woman's eyelashes, Rachel's heart melted within her. She steered Melissa to the settle, went after a mug of coffee for her trembling guest, then sat in the rocker facing her. "How can I help you?" she asked after giving the woman time to collect herself.

Melissa hiccupped twice, then sat quietly for another moment, gathering strength. Then she leaned forward. "Homer is too hard on our children. He hurts me too. Oh, Rachel, what can I do?" She pulled her long sleeve above her elbow, exposing a dark bruise.

"Did he do that?" Rachel asked, horrified.

"Yes, he does it continually. The children are bruised and their backs have long red welts most of the time. What can I do, Rachel? I have to protect my children."

VERALEE WIGGINS is the author of many novels, including *Llama Lady* and *Sweet Shelter*. Mrs. Wiggins makes her home in Washington State.

Books by VeraLee Wiggins

HEARTSONG PRESENTS

HP17—Llama Lady
HP33—Sweet Shelter
HP76—Heartbreak Trail
HP83—Martha My Own
HP92—Abram My Love

The Misplaced Angel

VeraLee Wiggins

The Forerunners/Book Four
A sequel to *Heartbreak Trail*

Heartsong Presents

For you, Bob and Ginger.

I love you oh so much.
Because you do the neatest things
And always keep in touch.

A note from the Author:
I love to hear from my readers! You may write to me at
the following address: **VeraLee Wiggins**
                            Author Relations
                            P.O. Box 719
                            Uhrichsville, OH 44683

ISBN 1-55748-711-1

THE MISPLACED ANGEL

Cover illustration by Kathy Arbuckle.

PRINTED IN THE U.S.A.

one

Rachel Dorland dropped the diaper she'd been scrubbing, shook dirty water from her hands, and straightened up. Her right hand moved to her aching back which she massaged as best she could. "Why are you causing your mama so much discomfort already, baby? I hardly knew Tommy was there at eight months."

Rachel grinned and shook her red head. "And how come I'm talking to it already?" she asked herself out loud. Washing her hands in the bowl, she dried them and went to check on her eleven-month-old son Tommy. *Sleeping soundly. What a fantastic baby! Whoever said children caused so much work must not have liked babies.* Rachel did and couldn't wait for her second one to arrive, hopefully a girl.

She finished the washing, hung the washboard on the nail outside the back door, hung the clothes on the line in spite of the drippy sky, cleaned up the house, then herself. *Not bad,* she thought, checking the clock. *Just time to play the piano a few minutes before making Tom's dinner.*

Sitting down on the padded bench, she ran through a few chords, remembering how badly she'd wanted to bring her piano from Illinois. Papa had made her leave it with Grandmother as it was so heavy the oxen couldn't pull it. She hadn't believed him at first, but as others left their treasures by the trail and oxen started dying in their yokes, she understood. The Trail claimed legions of animals. She'd always loved animals so much that she was glad she had not caused any to sacrifice their lives, even for her beloved piano.

She played Schubert's "Serenade" twice, giving her entire self to the haunting melody. Then lifting her bulky body, she hurried to the kitchen where she made a thick, creamy potato soup and slathered sweet-cream butter onto fluffy homemade bread.

At 12:45 Tom burst through the door. "Sorry I'm late," he said, kissing her on the forehead. Then he smiled tenderly and hugged her properly. "How's my round little mama today?" he asked. Rachel, who stood only an inch over five feet, truly looked as wide as she did tall.

Rachel returned her thin five-foot, nine-inch husband's hug. She loved him so much, even more than when they'd married nearly two years ago, back in '59, fresh off the Oregon Trail. She loved God more now too. At the end of the long trail, Heartbreak Trail she'd called it, she'd finally accepted Jesus' great sacrifice for her. Since then as she'd read His precious Word and seen Him working in her life, she'd learned to love Him more and more. She'd also grown more in love with Tom as the days passed.

Lots had happened since then. They'd built a cabin in Oregon City, but had lived in it only until Tom had developed a good practice—and they could afford the house they lived in now.

The large house had a beautiful kitchen with a shiny black cook stove, a dining room they never used, and a large front room they always used. Upstairs they had three large bedrooms. They slept in one with Tommy beside their bed in his lovely cherry wood crib. A beautiful matching cradle on the other side of the bed waited for the new baby. Rachel had set up the new sewing machine in one of the other bedrooms and boxes of church material cluttered the room. The third bedroom, empty now, would one day be filled with their children.

Tom and Rachel hadn't taken a land donation claim because they had know he'd be more than busy with his doctoring. His practice of medicine was what had first brought them together on the wagon train, and they had learned to know each other as she'd helped him care for the sick and injured people on the wagon train. He'd also cared for the animals, which endeared had him to her. She'd planned to help him after they married and she did—as often as they could get her father Nate Butler to watch Tommy. Rachel enjoyed helping Tom and he relished having her with him.

"This is good—and warming," Tom said now, sampling the soup. "It's not exactly raining out there, but it's damp and cold. I guess this weather isn't unusual for August here in the Willamette Valley." They ate in quiet contentment for a few minutes. "How's the back?" he soon asked. "Any better?"

Rachel shook her head. "I spent two hours bending over the wash tub this morning. That didn't suit the baby much. I think it felt crowded. In fact, I can tell it's a huge baby. My stomach's so tight I don't see how it can stretch another bit." She peered into Tom's eyes. "You don't think it could be another boy, do you?"

Tom laughed out loud. "Rachel, I've been telling you, it has a fifty percent chance of being a boy."

She shook her shiny auburn head. "No, because Tommy's a boy. He had a fifty percent chance of being a boy. Now we get the other fifty percent chance."

He turned from the table and pulled her into his lap. "I'll tell you once again, love, and try to listen. Each baby has the same chance of being a boy or girl. You think the baby's big, so it could easily be a boy."

Rachel started to object, but a small cry from the crib interrupted her. Tom picked up Tommy and plopped him into his mother's arms. The tiny boy flopped back, turned himself toward her body, and began searching for his meal.

As Rachel arranged him and began nursing him, Tom

smiled. "Seems hard to believe you're having another baby already. Tommy still seems like our little baby—but soon we'll have two. I hope it doesn't put his nose out of joint."

That afternoon Rachel sat at her new sewing machine and made several small dresses. Not for her baby that was on its way. She'd finished making clothes for the new baby over a month ago. These clothes were for needy children. Her Ladies' Aid group had asked her to sew them when she'd gotten the sewing machine. She was the only one in the area with one of the wonderful inventions, so she gladly helped. But this particular day, pedaling the thing seemed to aggravate her back. She stuck to the work until she finished, though, thinking she might not be able to do much more until after the baby came.

By evening she could hardly prepare supper. Good thing she'd put on beans right after dinner. Tom helped with Tommy until someone pounded on the door.

"Old man Craighill's horse threw him a while ago," the winded man said. "Better get on over there. I hear he ain't breathin' too good."

Tom assured him he'd go right over, and the man left. Tom looked at Rachel and sighed. "I wanted to put you to bed and take care of you tonight," he told her. Grabbing his black bag, he kissed her and took off trotting down their wooden sidewalk.

❧

The next morning Rachel had just finished washing the breakfast dishes when two women arrived with another box of material. "Several new families have just come in," said one of the women, Mrs. Gump, wiping the rain from her hair, "and they don't have nothing. Could you run up some shirts, pants, and dresses today?"

Rachel's heart dropped. She'd counted on taking it as easy as possible today. Last night her back had ached so badly she'd hardly slept. She hadn't gotten any sleep at all until after four-thirty when Tom had come home all broken up because he couldn't save Mr. Craighill.

"I'd like to help you, but I don't feel very well today," she said. "I may not be able to do any more until after the baby comes."

The tall, spare woman shook her head. "These have to be done today, Mrs. Dorland. You'd never believe how those poor little tykes are dressed—and the weather's just like winter. Why don't you hurry and get them done so you can rest a bit after the baby comes?"

Inasmuch as you have done it for the least of these, you've done it for Me. Every time someone wanted Rachel to do something that verse popped into her mind. Reluctantly, she accepted the material and patterns, took them to the long table, and started cutting. Somehow this wasn't as much fun as when she'd first gotten the machine. But she'd felt better then.

After lunch another woman came from the Ladies' Aid. "I suppose you know old man Craighill died," she told Rachel, then went on, not allowing her to say how awful Tom felt about the fine man's accident and death. "We're fixing some food for after the funeral. We thought we'd collect it and you can cook it."

"I'm not sure I'll be able to," Rachel said. "I'm not feeling too well today."

The woman tossed her gray head. "Well, it's not until tomorrow anyway. With that fancy cook stove of yours, won't be nothing to it. Thanks, Mrs. Dorland. We're shore glad you live here."

After the woman left, Rachel looked around at her house. It was definitely one of the nicest in Oregon City, maybe in all of Oregon. The two-story house had plastered walls and wool rugs on all the floors except the kitchen. Last spring

Rachel had been delighted when Tom told her they'd have a nice house built. And they'd been happy to share their home with the church family, having potlucks and other doings here when it rained—which, they'd discovered, was most of the time in Oregon City.

Rachel sighed and pulled the first piece of material from the box—heavy, dark blue jean, for children's clothes. An hour later, after leaning over the table cutting clothes, her back forced her to lie down for a few minutes.

The next thing she knew she felt herself being gently shaken. Opening her eyes, she discovered Tom leaning over her, kissing her gently. After sleeping so hard, she felt disoriented, not knowing whether it was day or night. "It's all right," his soft voice assured her. "This is a good place for you right now."

Then she remembered. *The church women—all that material. It must be noon,* she realized. "Where's Tommy?" she asked.

"Sleeping." He grinned. "You really fell asleep. What are all those pieces of material on the kitchen table?"

Rachel groaned, then changed it to a grin. "The ladies from the Aid brought them for me to sew for a poor family."

He looked at her thoughtfully. "I don't think you should do anymore than you have to right now, Rachel. The way you've been feeling, you could have the baby early. We don't want that."

She nodded. "I tried to tell them I didn't feel well. Oh well, the Lord will give me strength. Let's get you something to eat."

When Tom left, Rachel did the dishes and hurried to the sewing. She worked hard, finishing several pairs of pants and shirts, but that barely started the huge job.

As Rachel lay in bed that night trying to fall asleep, she felt little kicks and pokes all over her body, some of them strong enough to produce pain. She lovingly caressed her large, tightly-stretched stomach. "I think you must be an octopus in there," she whispered to her unborn baby. "Dear Father God, thank You for giving me such a beautiful family. Thank You for taking such good care of us, Father. Please help me to take especially good care of this tiny baby inside me. Thank You, Father, in Jesus' precious name. Amen."

When Rachel next opened her eyes, the night had given way to another dark and rainy day. She hurried through Tommy's bath so she could get at the sewing again. She must get that finished as soon as possible. She giggled. She'd hate to have to get up as soon as the baby was born and start sewing again.

She stayed with the sewing until dinnertime, though her back ached fiercely. A few minutes after Tom left on his rounds, Rachel began sewing again, but the women from the Ladies' Aid Society interrupted, bringing potatoes, parsnips, cabbage, onions, carrots, dried apples, and flour. They also handed her three bloody sacks containing meat.

"We brung everthing you'll need," the tall, hawk-like Mrs. Gump said. "Even apples for pies. You don't need to have the stuff finished until four o'clock. Oh yes, we baked the bread this morning so you wouldn't have much to do. We'll be back after the things."

Rachel sighed. "Help me, Father," she whispered. "You promised to be with us and not give us more than we could bear." She made the pies first, then the other things while the pies cooked. She tried her best to make everything attractive and tasty.

She managed to have the food ready when the women came after it. "You're an angel," one of the women said, giving Rachel a pat on the shoulder.

She went back to her sewing, but after only a few minutes she felt a pain, almost as if she needed to go to the bathroom. When it happened again fifteen minutes later, she watched the clock as she sewed. Four more came exactly fifteen minutes apart. "Oh no, Lord," she said aloud, "it's too early. Please, Father, let my pains stop. My baby isn't ready to be born yet." But the pains marched relentlessly on.

By the time Tom arrived for supper, the pains had increased in strength and came every ten minutes. After examining her, he told her the baby was definitely coming. "If you feel like it, you can help me box up all this stuff the women brought. You won't be doing anything like that for some time now. Then we'll prepare the bed."

They soon had the house ready and clothes and blankets laid out for the baby. Tom fixed some bread and fried venison sandwiches which they enjoyed between pains. He also took care of Tommy, except for nursing. "What am I going to do about Tommy?" Rachel wailed. "I planned to wean him during the next month."

Tom shook his sandy blond head. "Think you could nurse them both for awhile? I've seen tiny calves sucking from the same cows as yearlings."

Rachel's heart ached for the baby boy who'd have to give up nursing far too young. "I don't know. I'd be willing to try."

Tom smiled and gently smoothed her flaming hair away from her flushed face. "Let's do that at least for a little while. Don't worry, love, it'll all work out." Just then a wail from the crib reminded Rachel they had no one to care for her precious little boy during the birth. Tommy might be all right for that long—and he might not. They really needed someone to help them.

"Think you'd have time to get Papa?" she asked Tom. "Tommy likes him almost better than me."

Tom shook his head. "There's probably plenty of time," he said softly. "But you never know for sure. Unless a neighbor stops by that we could ask to help, we'd better just hope Tommy'll be all right. It'll probably be several hours before the baby comes and far past his bedtime." He leaned down and kissed her gently. "Shall we chance it?"

"I guess." *Oh, Lord,* she prayed silently, *please send someone to help with Tommy. I'm sorry we're so disorganized, but we didn't expect this for almost another month. Thank You, Lord. We'll be waiting for the one You want to care for Tommy. And help our new little baby be all right. Help it not be too small. Thank You, Lord. I love You.*

Another half hour passed and no one came to help. The pains had increased to every five minutes, and they were hard and strong now. If only Martha Lawford, Rachel's best friend from the wagon train, were here. She could make any baby happy.

"Think you can nurse Tommy now?" Tom asked. "If you can, he might be all right until after the baby's born."

Just then someone knocked on the door. "Not tonight," Tom said. "We can't have any company tonight."

Then Rachel remembered. "You'll have to answer it, Tom. I asked God to send someone to help with Tommy, and I guess she's here."

Tom scooped up Tommy and laid him in bed beside Rachel. "Try to nurse him between pains." He took off down the stairs, three at a time.

Rachel barely got Tommy started nursing when another pain struck. It hurt. It really hurt, but she held still so the little boy could get his last meal for a while.

Before the pain ended, Tom reappeared, a wide smile on his face. "It was the answer to your prayer, all right. Your father's downstairs. As soon as you finish there, I'll carry the crib and Tommy down. Now we know Tommy's in good hands."

"We have an incredible God who hears our cries, don't

we?" Rachel replied, feeling an intense peace within her. "I'm so glad He sent Papa instead of someone else. Oh, Tom, take Tommy. Another pain's coming."

Tom grabbed the crib, put the sleeping baby into it, and set it outside the bedroom door. "Come and get Tommy, Father Butler!" Tom called. He quickly shut the door and turned to help his wife.

A half hour later Tom laughed out loud. "It's a boy, Rachel, and he's not too small." He hurriedly wrapped the baby in a warm blanket. "About seven pounds I think. I'll get my scales in a little while." He turned the baby head down, reached a finger into its mouth, and cleaned out all the mucous he could reach. Then he laid the squalling baby in Rachel's arms and turned his attention to caring for her.

After a few minutes Rachel felt another strong pain. "The afterbirth must be coming," she said.

Then another even stronger pain forced Rachel to lay the baby on the bed. "Something's wrong, Tom. Something's hurting me real bad."

Tom worked another few seconds. "Push, love!" he suddenly yelled. "Push hard. There's another baby!"

two

Rachel pushed hard as Tom instructed and soon he held another baby in his big hands, cleaning mucous from its mouth and throat. "What is it?" Rachel asked. "Why isn't it crying?"

Tom met her eyes and smiled. "I guess it isn't as mad about being born as the first one was." He smiled some more. "The baby's fine but I'm afraid to tell you what it is."

Rachel dropped her head to the pillow. "Another boy," she said softly.

Tom nodded. "But he's a beaut." After Tom looked the babies over and did the necessary things for them, he laid them both beside Rachel, then cut a piece of red material from the church's box and tied it around one tiny ankle. Shuffling through the box again, he found a piece of yellow, which he cut and tied around one of the other baby's minute legs.

"Why did you do that?" Rachel asked. "Something's wrong, isn't it?" She held the still-squalling baby to her breast. He knew exactly what to do. She smiled into Tom's eyes. "That's what he wanted. Why did you tie those things around their ankles?"

Tom kissed his tired wife. "I did it to help us tell the babies apart. We know which was born first because he cried and the other didn't. Tomorrow we might never know which was which. I think the babies are identical, Rachel."

Rachel suddenly felt desperately tired. "Tell Papa," she whispered as she drifted into a happy sleep.

❧

Rachel awakened suddenly, wondering where she was—then remembered: she had two brand new little boys. "Thank You, precious Lord," she whispered. "Thank You for bringing my babies safely into the world." She grinned sheepishly. "And thank You, God, for giving me exactly what I wanted—boys. I didn't know but You did. Oh, Father, You're so good. I love You so much. And thank You for sending Papa to care for Tommy." She looked around but found no one in her room, not Tom, not Tommy, not two tiny babes. Where were they all? Were they all right?

Just then the door of her bedroom eased open, and Tom's eye peeped through the crack. When Rachel waved, he came in, a big smile sprawling across his face. He leaned over the bed and kissed her gently. "How do you feel?" he whispered.

"I'm fine," Rachel said clearly. "Why are we whispering? And where are my litter of babies?"

Tom pointed at the door. "Father Butler's been entertaining Tommy. The other two have been sleeping for the last three hours."

"Three hours? Have I been sleeping that long? Well, I feel pretty good. Could I see Tommy?"

A moment later Tom sat the eleven-month-old baby on the bed beside Rachel. Tommy barely accepted her hugs before sliding down beside her, looking for lunch. Her eyes flew to Tom's. "Shall I nurse him?"

He shrugged. "This milk will have the little babies' colostrum, but I guess Tommy'll have to use it too." As she nursed Tommy, Tom appeared to be deep in thought. Finally he nodded. "Yes, I think you should keep nursing him if you have plenty for everyone, but let's start pushing milk from a glass and table food to him. What do you think?"

She shook her head. "I don't know. Feeding twins seems like a miracle, but I don't want Tommy to feel pushed aside.

I'm willing to try." She motioned toward the door. "Could you get Papa?"

When Nate Butler came in, Rachel wanted to get out of bed and run to him. The dearest father in the world who'd always been there for her. She pulled the sheet over the nursing baby and held out her arms for his welcome hug.

"Looks as how you're nursing the wrong baby, aren't you?" Nate asked.

Rachel nodded. "I think so. I feel guilty nursing him but I'll feel guilty if I don't. We shouldn't have had these babies so soon." She looked at Tom. "Have you weighed them yet? Are they big enough to be all right?"

"Don't worry, love. The babies are perfectly healthy. Number one weighs six pounds, two ounces, and number two weighs six pounds, three ounces. They're both twenty inches long. Father Butler and I've gone over those babies carefully and we can't find any difference in them."

Unable to resist seeing what was going on, Tommy gave up nursing and scrambled from under the sheet. He looked from his papa to his grandpa and back to his mama, then burst into wild laughter. Rachel hugged her silly precious baby.

Tom hurried to the kitchen and returned with a bit of milk in a glass. Taking Tommy in his arms, he put the glass to the baby's mouth and tipped it up. Tommy, eager to try something new, choked on the milk but tried again as soon as he could breathe.

"I want to see my babies," Rachel said. "Could you get them for me, Papa?" She shook her head and laughed softly. "Imagine three babies under a year! How am I ever going to manage?"

Nate brought the babies in and laid them beside Rachel. "You'll manage. I can help you sometimes." His eyes grew red and he blinked hard a few times. "If Alma had lived she could have given you all the help you need."

"That's the first thing I thought of, Papa. Wouldn't Mama have loved our babies?" She held first one over her stomach, then the other. Finally one awakened and fussed so, Rachel put him under the sheet where Tommy had been and tried to nurse him. He fussed louder but refused to take the nipple. Rachel smiled at her father. "I'm sorry, Papa, but could you go out for now? Looks like this one doesn't know how to eat."

Tom took Tommy out too so Rachel threw back the sheet and taught baby number two how to get a meal. When he caught on he nursed hungrily for ten minutes. She held him over her stomach and burped him, then laid him down and nursed baby number one. This baby didn't have to be taught anything. He was too hungry. After ten minutes he fell asleep also, so she burped him over her stomach and laid him down, then rolled on her side so she could touch them, fondle them, just look at them.

She tried her best to see some difference in the babies but couldn't. Both had lots of fluffy brown hair, even on their backs. Both had smoky blue eyes—but they could turn any color in the next few months. Both had perfect little rosebud mouths, not too big and not too small. Both little noses turned up just a tiny bit on the end. All ten little fingers looked wide and chubby, and all four fat little legs looked exactly alike, with huge feet wiggling at the end. The babies truly looked alike. They even looked exactly the same size.

What beautiful babies Tom and I make. Then she remembered God. *Oops. Sorry, Father. I know You made them. But You made them from both of us. What a glorious gift You've given us, Lord, helping You in Your job of creation. Thank You, God. Help us care for them exactly the way You want us to. You know best. You always know best.*

After a while a small knock sounded on the door. "Sorry," she said after inviting her father and husband in, "I'm enjoying them so much I forgot all about you two—I mean three."

Nate, now holding Tommy, sat in the rocker, and Tom, after kissing her again, sat on the edge of the bed. "You have a big job to do right away," he said, his eyes aglow with love—and happiness. "We have to think of two more names in the near future. In the meantime I'll make a midnight supper. Are you hungry?"

Rachel hadn't thought about it, but she definitely felt hungry. Really hungry. "Yes, fix everything we have in the house."

Tom laughed and patted her shoulder. "I'll probably have to if you're nursing three growing boys." He got up, started toward the door, then returned to the bed to take her hand. "Tommy loved drinking from the glass, though. It'll all work out."

Her heart overflowed with love for her kind husband. "I know. And God helped my milk last long enough for all three at least once. He'll take care of us." She kissed Tom's hand and released it.

While Tom and Papa fixed the meal, Rachel thought about names. They'd already chosen one boy's name, Jesse. What could the other one be? Should it be like Jesse? Or really different?

Tom and Papa soon brought supper in for all three of them. They moved the small table from under the window and set it up beside the bed. "We wanted to eat together," Tom said. Tom and Papa took turns feeding Tommy potatoes, mashed dried peas, mashed carrots, and finely chopped roast meat. "See? He loves to eat!" Tom said. "He'll soon forget all about nursing."

Rachel didn't answer but felt a pang of guilt. She wasn't

sure she wanted her first baby to forget their special bond yet. She ate all she could hold and drank a tall glass of milk, then fell asleep again.

Tommy insisted on nursing again, and Rachel once again felt guilty. Would she have enough for the little babies? She breathed a sigh of relief when Tommy fell asleep. He always slept all night, but she had no idea what the new babies would do.

Papa decided to stay the night in case all three babies gave trouble. He slept on the settle in the front room.

Baby one awakened at eleven o'clock, screaming to nurse. He barely finished when baby two awakened and fussed quietly. Tom picked him up. "I think you're going to have to do better than that around here," he told the baby who'd quieted as soon as he felt Tom's arms. "It's liable to get pretty noisy," he added gently, placing the baby beside Rachel on the bed.

The baby remembered what he was supposed to do, nursed, and fell asleep in Rachel's arms. Tom put him back in the cradle beside his brother.

At one o'clock in the morning baby number one woke again, screaming as loud as he could. Tom got him for Rachel who nursed him. He fell asleep but awakened when Tom put him back in the cradle and yelled at the top of his lungs. Once again he nursed and fell asleep—and once again he wakened when Tom put him in the cradle with his brother.

Rachel felt so tired she could barely nurse the baby. "Maybe we should let him sleep with us," she said.

Tom looked pretty tired too as he put the baby beside Rachel and climbed into bed.

The baby slept for an hour, then began wiggling. In another minute he began screaming almost as loud as Tommy could. Rachel pulled him to her breast. He sampled the milk, opened his mouth, and bellowed again. Rachel laid him over her stomach and patted his back. He still yelled. "Be still, baby," she whispered gently caressing his soft hair. "You'll wake Papa and Tommy." He still bellowed.

After a few minutes Tom stirred. "Rachel," he said softly, "the baby's hungry."

"No," Rachel said. "He's just trying to wake the household. Could you bring me a diaper please?"

Tom staggered to the pile of flannel diapers and moved several to the bed. "You're going to have to make more diapers," he said, then grinned. "I'll bet we're about one baby short on clothes."

Rachel changed the baby, wrapped him tight in a soft blanket, and tried to nurse him again, but he still yelled. "Do you think something's wrong with him?" she finally asked fearfully.

"I don't think so. Let me try walking with him." Tom walked around the room cuddling the baby; he quieted right down.

Rachel fell asleep thirty seconds after the room became quiet. She faintly heard a small cry but it stopped right away so she slept on. Some time later she woke with a start to find Tom still walking with the baby on his shoulder. "Why don't you put him down now?" she asked. "You can't do that all night."

Tom managed a tired smile. "I tried, love, several times, but he knows a good thing when he finds it."

"But you need your sleep."

"Not as much as you. You go back to sleep and get rested."

Baby one spent most of the night in Tom's arms. Baby two woke once to nurse and fell back to sleep before he finished. Tommy slept through all the commotion.

The next morning Rachel felt good. Tom looked awful and baby one still wanted to be held.

"I'm glad your father's still here," Tom said after preparing breakfast, cleaning up afterward, and bathing three babies. Baby one as well as baby two had fallen asleep after the bath and seemed to be sleeping soundly. "I have a few house calls I can't delay. Should I try to get a woman to come in?"

Nate made shooing motions. "What can a woman do that I can't? You just go do what you have to and don't worry about a thing."

Tom hadn't been gone long when Rachel heard someone knock on the front door. Nate opened the door.

"Is Rachel here?" she heard Mrs. Gump ask. "We're here to pick up the clothes she made yesterday."

"I don't think she got them done because—" Nate began.

But the woman interrupted. "She must have finished at least part of them. I told her we'd need them badly this morning. Could you please get her, Mr. Butler? This is very important to some ill-clad children."

Rachel thought she heard Papa laugh. *Oh, Mrs. Gump would think Papa didn't even care.*

"Well, I think Rachel's pretty busy right now," Papa said. "And as for ill-clad children, I think she needs some help herself."

Even from the bedroom, Rachel heard Mrs. Gump draw in a breath. "Is Rachel here, Mr. Butler? If she is please ask her to come to the door."

Papa had the nerve to laugh again, Rachel felt certain he did. "She can't come to the door, but I'm sure she wouldn't mind if you came up to see her for a moment. Come in, won't you?"

A moment later Papa knocked on the half-open door and ushered the woman into Rachel's bedroom. "You have company, Rachel. She won't stay long."

The woman looked shocked to find Rachel in bed. "What's wrong?" she asked.

Rachel laughed gleefully. "Nothing's wrong, Mrs. Gump.

You knew I was about to have a baby, didn't you?"

"Yes, I guess you are. Oh! Did you have it?"

"Yes, Mrs. Gump. In fact, I had twins. They're in the cradle over there."

The woman looked at the babies for a moment, then returned to Rachel. "I guess everyone's all right?"

"Yes. Everyone's just fine, thank you. Tired but fine."

"I see. I'm sorry to bother you right now, but did you get those clothes finished? We really need them."

"I got a few finished, but the babies started coming pretty early and I had to quit." She turned to Nate. "Papa, could you get those things in that box over by the wall for Mrs. Gump?"

He handed the small stack of children's clothes to the woman. "There you are. I'm amazed she got this many finished, Mrs. Gump. She's very dedicated."

The woman looked at the clothes as if to see if they were good enough, turned to go, then came back to Rachel. "When will you be able to get back to your sewing, do you suppose?"

"I'm not sure. I'm going to be awfully busy with three babies less than a year old."

"We're all busy," Mrs. Gump replied. "We just have to remember God asks us to go beyond our family to serve Him. Good-bye, Rachel. Good luck, and let me know when you have more clothes made."

Papa let her out and closed the door before exploding. "I don't believe what I just heard," he said loudly. "Not, 'What can we do for you?' but 'Get out of that bed and start sewing.' You just don't worry a second about her, Rachel."

"But she's right, Papa. God does expect us to help those less fortunate than us. The Bible says so."

"The Bible doesn't mean you right now," Papa said. "You notice most of the people who are out helping others have their own families raised. I'm not putting them down, understand. They're doing a great thing for God. But right now, she should have offered to help you. You're going to be busier than anyone you know."

When Tom came home for lunch, Nate had prepared a big vegetable soup which everyone eagerly ate, even Tommy. "See?" Tom said. "He's willing to be a big boy."

"Tell Tom about the woman," Nate said to Rachel.

"Well, Mrs. Gump came after the clothes and wasn't too happy when they weren't finished."

Tom pointed at the cradle with the two sleeping babies. "Did she see that?"

"Yes, but you know what? She didn't even ask if they were boys or girls or about their names or anything at all."

Tom gathered her close in his arms. "Don't you worry about that old busybody. Forget the whole world, Rachel, and let's just take care of our own three babies right now. That's a big enough job for a strong woman, Rachel, let alone one who's just gone through childbirth." He took her hand and eased himself to a seat on the bed beside her. "Now, let's talk about names for our babies."

"We already had Jesse. Should we go ahead and use that name? Or do you want to find two matching ones?"

He shook his head. "Let's not have matching names. Let's let our little boys be individuals. I'd even prefer not to dress them alike, at least not all the time."

Rachel nodded. "Okay, baby two is Jesse. Is that all right?"

Tom smiled. "It's fine, but you skipped baby one. Why isn't he Jesse?"

Rachel laughed. "He needs a big tough name, like Thor or Samson."

Tom shook his head. "Not necessarily. Maybe he's going to be a sissy. He cries all the time, you know."

Rachel turned over, searching for a comfortable position.

"This is hard, isn't it? It would have been easier if we'd named them before they were born."

"Right." Tom got up, leaned over, and kissed her. "You just keep thinking about it. The name will come to one of us and it'll be right. I need to see two more people. Then I better try washing clothes for three babies."

Tommy napped and so did Rachel while Papa washed dishes and heated water for washing clothes. Rachel could hardly stay in bed as she listened to the two men trying to wash the clothes. Although they obviously didn't know what they were doing, they finally got the little clothes on the line.

Papa came in shaking his head. "I had no idea what you women go through washing clothes and running a house."

Tom soon appeared looking tired. He sat on the bed, leaned over, and nuzzled her face. "How are you, love?" he asked. "Pretty well worn out?"

She hugged him. And loved him more than she could have ever imagined. "I'm not as tired as you," she said. "Maybe I should get up and help you."

"No way. Your job is to feed these babies and to think up a name—a tough name."

In the midst of talking quietly, Tom dropped off to sleep. Rachel eased his head to the bed beside her. Now, if she could just keep three babies happy he could get a short rest. She knew it would never happen though as baby one never went a half hour without letting his presence be felt. And Tommy seemed to be demanding more attention than usual, probably because things were so different. Thank goodness, Papa took care of Tommy most of the time.

She lay quietly thinking of names. The name Jesse meant God's gift. They needed another name as precious but more powerful—baby one was going to be somebody tough and strong. She fell asleep with Tom and they both slept a peaceful hour before baby one demanded his meal.

When baby one was fed and changed, Tommy awakened and wanted to nurse. Tom took him out to the kitchen and tried to feed him some soup and milk, but he wouldn't stop crying long enough to try any. Tom soon brought him in, and as Rachel nursed him she wondered why he looked so enormous lying in the bed.

Then she knew. She was comparing him to his new brothers. She'd been looking at those two tiny babes a lot during the last few hours. As Tommy nursed, his eyes never left Rachel's. He reached for her nose, smiled and laughed, sometimes losing the nipple. What a difference! Those two little ones never even opened their eyes while they fed but tended to the serious business of turning themselves into full-grown men.

The night was a repeat of the night before. Baby one spent most of the night in Tom's arms as he walked about the house. Tommy slept all night and Jesse awakened once at four o'clock to nurse, then fell fast asleep again.

As Rachel listened to Tom walking baby one and trying to keep him quiet, she had a terrible thought. Maybe they should name the baby Lucifer, the most beautiful angel in heaven who became the devil. "I was just kidding, Lord," she whispered into the darkness. "I love my baby and even if I didn't I'd never name anything Lucifer, not even a bad horse."

Name him Gabriel, Rachel. That means sent from God. All three of your babies were, you know.

Gabriel! She'd have never thought of that name in a million years. And there could never be a more powerful name! The next time Tom and baby one wandered into the bedroom, Rachel told him about the name Gabriel. He nodded sleepily. "Sure. If you like Gabriel, so do I."

"Tom! I didn't suggest Gabriel. God did. I think we'd better listen to Him, don't you?"

"Sure. Hey, do you think Gabriel would nurse and fall asleep?"

She took the baby, changed him, and glanced toward Tom. Poor dear. He'd fallen asleep already. Gabriel nursed as if he'd never had a meal in his life. Rachel giggled. He hadn't had very many. But he would. Oh, he would. With his disposition he'd have most anything he wanted.

Gabriel fell asleep after nursing about ten minutes and so did Rachel. A half hour later, though, the baby roused, and Rachel tried in vain to nurse him. When she couldn't quiet him, she gingerly climbed from her bed, put him over her shoulder, and walked around the room. He snuggled close and quieted. She sat in the rocker and every time he stirred she awakened enough to give a few rocks, back and forth, back and forth. It worked and she managed to sleep most of the night. Jesse awakened at four o'clock again, nursed, and fell asleep.

"Why couldn't you be like that?" she asked Gabriel as she rocked him again at five o'clock.

The days and nights continued nearly the same for the first week. By that time Rachel did most of the night duty and some of the day work, but slept whenever she could. She felt stronger every day and each day learned better how to handle the added work. She even managed to play the piano for a few minutes once in a while, something that brought her great joy.

"You're doing too much," Tom said. But Rachel thought it a pretty weak reprimand. No wonder. Back at his doctoring full time, and helping a lot at home besides, she needed to be doing her own work, as much as possible and as soon as possible.

Papa had to go home to catch up on his blacksmithing, a trade he'd brought from Illinois where they used to live, but he appeared at some time every day to chop wood, wash dishes or clothes, or whatever Rachel needed.

When Gabe and Jesse were two weeks old, Mrs. Gump appeared again. "You're looking perty good," she said. "I was just wondering. You got those clothes finished yet?"

three

Rachel felt like closing the door, but instead she invited the woman inside. "I'm afraid I haven't even gotten my own sewing done yet," she said. "I have exactly half enough clothes for my new babies. I'm just starting to handle the work here. Papa and Tom still do a lot for me, so you can see it's quite impossible right now. You have no idea how much work three babies under a year are to care for. Would you like to take the material and give it to someone else? Or do it yourself?"

A quick scowl passed over Mrs. Gump's features. "No one else has a sewing machine," she said. "You know that, Rachel. That's why you must make time to do it. Soon."

Inasmuch as you have done it for the least of these, you've done it for Me. Oh, Lord, I love You so much, Rachel said silently. *You've done so much for me that I'd never turn You away. Never ever.*

Rachel smiled and nodded. "I will, Mrs. Gump. As soon as I possibly can. Would you like some tea? I haven't had the time or strength to do any baking yet."

The woman got to her feet, a satisfied smile settled in place. "I must be going, but I appreciate your helpful spirit. I'll be back in a few days for the clothes. Thanks again, dear. You're an angel."

As Rachel sat in the rocker nursing Gabe, she wondered exactly how she planned to make clothes for Mrs. Gump. Her family kept her far busier than her strength allowed. And how could she sew for someone else when Papa and Tom took so much time from their busy lives to help her?

29

Father God, what do You want me to do here? Should I sew those clothes for Mrs. Gump while Tom and Papa are still helping me? Is that fair to them? Or is it more important for me to sew the clothes no matter what? And we need more clothes for the twins too, really bad. Please, Father, show me what You want me to do.

Looking at the tiny face before her, Rachel suddenly realized Gabe must receive much more nourishment than Jesse. He ate three times to Jesse's two. She'd have to ask Tom if that was all right. Pondering her problems, Rachel fell asleep.

"Rachel, love, I'm sorry to wake you, but Jesse's fussing." Rachel opened her eyes to Tom's loving face.

She listened but couldn't hear anything. "Are you sure?" she asked fuzzily.

Tom gently took Gabe from her and replaced him with Jesse who eagerly accepted the offered meal. After putting Jesse in the cradle beside Gabe, Rachel wearily prepared supper. And ate it, too tired to care. But she had a big responsibility to three babies—so she ate.

የ

The next morning Rachel hurried through breakfast, dishes, three baths, and house cleaning. Then she rushed to her sewing machine to make children's clothes. Gabe interrupted at least every half hour, and Tommy needed lots of attention. He kept pulling himself up to her knees so she stopped pedaling for fear she'd pinch him.

Somehow she managed to get three little shirts made that day before she did the washing, which also took forever, working around three babies' demands.

Late in the afternoon someone knocked on the door. "Hello," Mrs. Gump sang out. "I just stopped by to pick up the clothes. I can't tell you how much they'll be appreciated."

Rachel felt positively undone. Her hair hung everywhere, her clothes were damp from wash water, and Gabe in her arms was wet and mussed too. She swallowed her impatience before answering the woman. "Just a minute and I'll get them," she said, hurrying to the bedroom for the things. "There you are," she said to the woman, who looked surprised.

"I thought you'd have them all finished," Mrs. Gump said. "I left the material here nearly three weeks ago, you know."

"How well I know," Rachel said. "That was the day the twins were born."

Mrs. Gump looked at Gabe in Rachel's arms. "Every time I come over you're holding the same baby," she said. "You did have two didn't you?"

Rachel laughed. "They look alike, Mrs. Gump, but they don't act alike. Tom and I can't even tell them apart when they're asleep." She really didn't need to explain anything more to Mrs. Gump, but somehow she found herself prattling on. "Tom put different colored ribbons around their legs when they were born so we wouldn't get them mixed up, but there's really no chance of that, their dispositions are so different."

Mrs. Gump suddenly jumped back, as if caught appearing interested in Rachel's child were dishonest or immoral. "Well, I must get on down the road. Shall I come back tomorrow for the rest of the things?"

Rachel shook her head. "Wait a week. You have no idea how hard I work." She glanced down at Gabe, sleeping as if he'd never think of keeping her awake. "And this baby keeps me up all night too. It's hard, Mrs. Gump."

"Humph. You shouldn't spoil the child like that, Rachel. Let him cry a few nights and he'll learn to sleep when he should."

Rachel opened her mouth but then closed it again. After a

moment, she said brightly, "I'm sure I'll have some more clothes finished in a week. Maybe not many, but some."

"We need them all—now," Mrs. Gump said, closing the door.

"Well," Rachel said to Tommy who needed changing and something to eat. "Think I better stop spoiling you boys?" She changed him, put him in the wooden high chair, and heated some left-over dried peas. Pouring in a little milk, she mashed them with a fork and offered him a spoonful. He took several spoonfuls, then cried. Every time she offered him more he batted the spoon away.

"Maybe you'll drink some milk from a glass," she said, pouring it. He drank two swallows, then turned his head, still crying. "Well, I guess you're still my little boy, aren't you?" She took him to the rocker and he emptied both breasts in five minutes. After letting him nurse a few more minutes anyway, she put him on the floor.

"Now I'll do some more sewing for the church," she said getting out the cut-out pieces. Just as she sat down to sew, Tommy pulled up to the chair and whimpered to be picked up. "I can't, babe," she said. "You heard the woman. She needs these clothes yesterday. Never mind if you go hungry and the twins go naked." She giggled and sat the little boy down a few feet from the chair and gave him his teething ring.

She'd sewed part of one seam when Gabe let out his usual roar. He'd nursed and been changed less than a half hour ago. Maybe she shouldn't pick him up every time he cried. She sewed a few more seams but the noisy baby seemed to be picking up steam. Rachel sighed and laid down the little shirt she'd been working on. If she didn't get Gabe he'd for sure wake up Jesse.

As soon as Gabe heard her coming he snuffled his yelling to a few hiccups, then a total stop. Rachel shook her head as she lifted him from the cradle. "You already know a lot, don't you?" she asked the tiny boy. He looked around as if he'd never seen the room before and also as if he'd never interrupt anyone ever.

She managed to have one shirt done by the time Tom came home for dinner. "Whatcha been doing?" he asked as he washed his hands.

"Mostly taking care of Gabe," she said. "And making one little shirt."

"That's good," Tom said. "If you could make a bunch more you might not have to wash every day."

Rachel hurried to put the potato soup and steak sandwiches on the table. "Well, the shirts weren't for our babies," she said. "Mrs. Gump came again and wasn't pleased that I hadn't made more clothes for her project."

"But you don't have time to sew for her right now," he objected. "You can't even keep up your own work yet."

Rachel put Tommy into his high chair and sat down before the steaming food. "I know, Tom, but you know what the Bible says, if you do it for the least of these you do it for Me."

Tom laughed. "That's right, but charity also begins at home. As for the least, don't you think our new boys would be considered the least? Which reminds me, I want to weigh them tonight. They're nearly a month old."

Rachel worked hard on the church things most of the afternoon. Then she washed clothes and made bread. They'd had only biscuits since the babies had come, and she knew Tom loved yeast bread. By the time she sat down to the supper table she felt far too tired to eat. Remembering her three babies, she ate all she could force down.

Tom weighed the babies that night and each had gained five ounces. "Not great by any means," he told Rachel, "but I think they're all right."

Every morning Rachel felt a little more tired than the day before, but she pushed ahead, picturing Mrs. Gump's unhappy face. She had nearly half the clothes done when the tall, thin woman arrived.

"I have a lot done this time," Rachel said, trying to sound cheerful.

But when Mrs. Gump saw the small bundle of clothes, she didn't return the smile. "If you didn't hold a baby all the time you could get other things done," she said sternly. "Well, I sincerely hope the rest will be finished next week."

"One more week," she told Tommy. "Then we'll just have ourselves to take care of." She gave the wiggly baby a hug. "Won't that be nice? I'll have more time to play with you. You have a birthday coming up too. Maybe I can make a cake."

Before the week ended, Gabe started crying fifteen minutes after he ate rather than a half hour, and Jesse became fussy too. Sensing the monumental changes in his world, Tommy wanted to nurse all the time, seeking comfort and reassurance as much as nourishment. After a few days of worsening conditions and more crying from all three, Rachel noticed her breasts never filled with milk anymore. She felt far too tired to deal with one more crisis.

"What can I do?" she asked Tom at dinnertime.

He shook his head. "We have to do what we tried to avoid. As of this minute Tommy is weaned. He'll survive but the twins won't." He watched Rachel a moment, then continued. "You have to get more rest, and eat and drink more. You're killing yourself trying to do so much, love."

"Tom, how can I nurse the twins in front of him? He's big enough to know what's going on."

He shook his head, looking sad. "Maybe you can cover yourself so he won't know."

It took Rachel an hour to get Tommy to sleep for his nap

without nursing. She rocked him but he twisted and turned, throwing himself back and forth in her lap, determined to nurse no matter what. Finally he cried himself to sleep in her arms. Then she managed to sew for an hour while all the babies slept. She kept falling asleep at the sewing machine. First her head would nod, then her feet would slow down and she'd wake up. *Oh, Father, how I'd love to nap while the boys do. But I'm doing this for You, so I won't complain.*

That night she fell into bed as soon as Tommy finished screaming himself to sleep. If she could just get a small rest before Gabe started up. Gabe had actually seemed a little quieter during the afternoon, and he'd slept quietly for more than an hour.

Tom awakened Rachel when he put the baby in bed beside her. "I'm so sorry to wake you," he whispered, "but he thinks he's starving."

The next few days went almost exactly like that one. Tommy refused table food and screamed himself to sleep every time. The babies eagerly took all Rachel's meager supply. Rachel barely got her housework done and the clothes washed. Tommy's birthday came and Rachel made a small cake. She was too tired to try a party and Tommy wouldn't touch the cake—or anything else.

"Don't worry about it, love," Tom said. "He wouldn't understand a birthday party anyway."

Rachel completely forgot about the church clothes until Mrs. Gump arrived asking for them. Rachel felt a huge relief when the disgruntled woman stomped off down the street. But she just had to get those clothes finished so she could forget them—and Mrs. Gump.

To Rachel's surprise a few days after she had quit nursing Tommy, Gabe began to sleep longer between nursings. And Jesse became his sweet self again. The babies hadn't been getting enough milk. Rachel drank a glass of milk every time she thought about it and ate all she could hold three times a day. Still she felt so tired she could barely stagger through her days.

After about five days, even Tommy began to accept his new method of getting nourishment. Rachel's world quieted a little, but caring and washing for three babies as well as Tom and herself kept her going from morning to night. Once again Mrs. Gump left Rachel's house empty-handed. But she'd been difficult enough that Rachel determined to finish those clothes and get rid of them and the woman once and for all.

Rachel forced herself to work on the clothes rather than rest, and work on the clothes rather than entertain Tommy, and work on the clothes rather than cuddle the babies, and work on the clothes rather than enjoy Tom's company.

The little babies began smiling, and both Tom and Rachel spent considerable time coaxing the precious expressions from them. Nevertheless, Rachel managed to discipline herself to sew enough that by the next week, Mrs. Gump carried the rest of the clothes away, completely pleased with Rachel and herself. "You're an angel," the woman said happily.

Rachel couldn't believe how unburdened she felt the next morning after bathing the three babies and cleaning her house. After dinner she put the babies all to sleep and crawled into her own bed for a nap too. She slept for two quick hours until Gabe yelled for his meal. She felt better all afternoon and even made a dried apple pie for supper.

"You look like my angel tonight," Tom said.

"I feel great," she said. "I took a nap today rather than sew."

The next morning Rachel finished her morning work and cut out more baby clothes. She'd been having a hard time getting by with clothes for one baby. She'd hurry and get them sewed, then be able to relax and take naps some more. She noticed she had more milk again and wished she could nurse Tommy. But she wouldn't go through weaning him again for anything in this world. He was forever a big boy now. In fact, he'd taken a step alone the day before.

She worked hard all that day and finished three gowns and a dozen diapers. That would help a lot, but she needed another dozen diapers badly. Sometimes she'd had to borrow diapers from Tommy for the babies in order to wash only once a day. Somehow she didn't like to put Tommy's well-worn diapers on her new little babies. Well, in a couple more days she'd have plenty of clothes for all of them.

"You're looking great," Tom said to her one day when he came home, all finished with his house calls. "I'll bet you've forgotten all about our dream of working together to help the sick."

Rachel smiled. She hadn't forgotten, only temporarily delayed the dream. "I remember," she said. "You don't want me to bring three babies along on your rounds do you?"

He shook his light brown head and kissed her. "I'm afraid that might not go over, but what about Father Butler? I suppose it's out of the question to ask him to take care of three babies."

For a moment it sounded marvelous to Rachel. Something completely different from her normal work. Then she remembered nursing the twins. "I'd love to," she said, "but the twins still need me often."

"We could come home between calls. Gabe's a lot better than he used to be. Don't you think he could go a couple hours between meals once in a while? I think the little babies didn't get enough to eat when Tommy nursed."

Tom didn't push it but Rachel thought about it sometimes. She'd thoroughly enjoyed helping him while they'd come West on the Trail. She'd continued after they'd married until Tommy was born. She smiled. Maybe part of the joy helping on the Trail was getting to know and love Tom. Of course it had been, but she'd enjoyed the doctoring too, a whole lot.

She watched the clock to see how long the babies usually waited between nursings. Jesse seemed to nurse about every three and a half hours, and Gabriel every two and a half. Much better. Jesse slept about seven hours straight each night too. Gabriel still woke several times, indignantly yelling for food. At least he fell asleep right away when he finished.

"Remember our talk about me working with you?" she asked one evening. "How much did you have in mind?"

He grinned and shrugged. "I'll take whatever you give me. How about one afternoon each week? We can stop and feed the babies once in the middle."

She nodded. "Sounds wonderful. We can start as soon as Papa can come watch the boys."

A week later, the newly-finished baby clothes all lay in their drawers, Papa had arrived to watch the babies, and Rachel couldn't wait to spend her first afternoon working with Tom. Finally they took off walking down the street, Tom's black bag in his hand.

"Let me brief you on our work for the day," he said. "First I have to remove stitches from a little boy who fell off a horse onto a sharp stump. He's fine but nervous. Then I have to see an older man who's been having swelling in his arms and legs. Then a baby who's not gaining weight." He shifted his bag to the other hand and reached for hers. "Will any of these cases bother you? How about the baby who's not gaining?"

Rachel felt higher than the fluffy white clouds overhead. Even the weather had cooperated for this day. Warm and sunny—in late September! She couldn't believe the thrill of walking down the street all alone with her husband. No babies, no one but the two of them. "None of it bothers me," she said. "I just hope I'll be able to help you."

"Here we are," Tom said. "This is the little boy. See if you can keep him calm."

The boy about four began to cry when he saw Tom. She knelt beside him and put her arms around him. "Did Doctor tell you this won't hurt?" she asked.

The small black head bobbed up and down. "Yes. But it still hurts."

What could she do? Then she remembered. "Do you know Jesus?"

He nodded again. "I know He loves me."

"Well, Jesus is the great God who made you. Jesus can do anything; did you know that? He told us He'd be with us always. He's with you right now. So let's ask Him to keep it from hurting." Tom had finished getting out his tools to remove the stitches and stood waiting. Rachel bowed her head and put her hand on the little boy's head. "Dear Great Father God," she began. "We all know what a great and wonderful God You are. You can make the sun and moon and stars so we know You can do anything. Your Book says You're with us all the time—every minute. Now we're asking You to be with Phil here and help him not to feel any pain when Doctor takes out the stitches. We ask in Jesus' precious name, Lord, and thank You for hearing and answering our prayer."

"All right," Tom said, "now that we've taken care of the pain, let's get these stitches out so you can get all well." He snipped the stitches and pulled them out with tweezers. He did it so fast that Rachel almost didn't see them come out. Tom straightened up and smiled at Phil. "They're all out. Jesus really kept me from hurting you, didn't He?"

"Yeah! He didn't even let you hurt me a little."

Rachel took his hand. "Let's thank Jesus for helping us, all right? Dear Jesus, thank You for helping Phil not to feel any pain right now. Thank You for loving us so much. We love You too, Lord Jesus. We pray in Your precious name. Amen."

They left a relieved and happy little boy and went on to their next patient. "Why is this man swollen, and what can you do for him?" Rachel asked as they neared the man's home.

"I'm sure you know how they treat these cases. They think he has too much blood so they take some out. The doctor who treated this man before me took out fourteen ounces. He didn't get better so the doctor took a whole quart. The man nearly died. As soon as he was able, he fired the doctor and sent for me."

four

Tom shook his head. "He'd heard that I don't believe in blood-letting. He was right. I don't. It doesn't make sense to take blood from someone who's sick. It always makes them weaker and I've seen doctors take so much the victim died almost immediately." He grinned. "Did you notice I didn't say patient?"

"Did you talk to the other doctor?"

He nodded. "I tried to tell him how wrong he is. But I'm one against the entire medical profession. I have a few other ideas that could cost me my medical license too, but I feel so strongly, I'll fight for my beliefs."

By this time they'd reached the man's house. The man's wife, Mrs. Daniels, welcomed them. Tom introduced Rachel as his helper, and they went in to visit the sick man.

"Say, Mr. Daniels, you look better. How do you feel?"

The plump little man smiled. "I feel better. Thanks to you. My poor wife's been spending most of her time gathering weeds for me to eat, but I think they're helping."

Tom nodded and turned to Mrs. Daniels. "You're being very careful to pick only the weeds I showed you, aren't you?"

"Yes, I am. I'm eating them too. I feel better too, and they's good."

Rachel smiled to herself, wondering what weed Tom had prescribed, and if it could really help a person.

Tom looked pleased. "Good for you. For both of you. Well, just keep doing what you are and I'll see you tomorrow."

"You told them to eat weeds?" Rachel asked when they

41

left the Daniels' place. "What are they? Are they really good to eat?"

Tom's eyes sparkled like the sun dappling through the hanging tree leaves. "I think so. My grandmother used to swear by the plant as a spring tonic. As soon as the weeds came up in the spring, Gran started pulling them. I never saw a sprier old woman than Gran. I know for sure they're better for a sick person than blood-letting or giving poison to make you vomit or give you diarrhea." He shook his head. "I can't figure out how trying to kill a person ever got recognition as a medical treatment."

They walked back home to check on the babies and Papa before the last call. Tommy and Papa were crawling all over the house together. Tommy enjoyed Papa so much he barely noticed Rachel and Tom's arrival. The twins slept soundly.

"Should we wake the babies and feed them?" Tom asked.

"We'd better or Papa may have a bad time in a few minutes." So she awakened Gabriel who eagerly gave up his nap for a warm meal. Jesse had a harder time waking up but he finally nursed too.

"Want to come on my last call?" Tom asked. "Or would you rather rest?"

"I want to come, Tom. This has been great fun. I learned a few things too, and have some things to think about." She quickly changed three diapers before they took off down the street together again.

After a half-mile walk they turned into a small home with a neat little yard. "How's Becky?" Tom asked when a young woman answered the door.

After the girl stepped back and invited them in, Tom introduced Rachel and told the girl she was his helper.

"Is Becky eating any better?" Tom asked as they followed her to the bedroom.

"I think so," the girl said. "I've been drinking a glass of

milk three times a day and drinking six glasses of water and eating all I can hold, just as you said. I can tell I have more milk—and as you predicted, Becky's more interested in nursing." She handed a tiny baby, much smaller than the twins, to Tom. "What do you think, Doctor?"

"She looks better for sure," Tom said. He laid the baby on the table and checked her over. "You just be sure to keep eating and drinking a whole lot, and she'll be all right."

The girl faced Rachel. "He's a great doctor," she said. "He had me feeding her sugar water for a day or two. She really latched onto it too. The other doctor wanted to feed her something to make her vomit and have diarrhea. He said she had indigestion and needed to be cleaned out. My husband wouldn't let me give the stuff to her."

"Good thing," Tom said. "This baby was nearly starved when I first saw her. I'm afraid that would have been the end. Good-bye now. I'll see you day after tomorrow."

"I do believe I'm married to a genius," Rachel said as they hurried back to their busy home. "Your patients seem to think so anyway."

"I'm not," Tom said. "But I do use a little common sense."

When they got home they found Papa awkwardly holding all three wide-awake babies, but nobody was crying. Tommy poked a finger into Gabe's mouth, which the baby eagerly sucked. Tommy looked up at his parents and giggled happily.

"How'd it go, Papa?" Rachel asked, taking the two small babies from him. "Think you could ever do it again?"

Papa nodded and laughed out loud. "Sure, I'll do it again."

Rachel heaved a sigh of relief. She'd really enjoyed going with Tom. Not that she helped him much, but she'd try harder next time.

"As soon as I forget what it's like," Papa finished with another chuckle. He reached for Rachel's hand. "I'm joking, daughter," he said. "The twins slept most of the time and I get along fine with Tommy."

Papa stayed for supper, then took off for his own small place.

⠀⠀⠀⠀⠀⠀⠀⠀⠀⠀⠀⠀⠀⠀♨

The next day Rachel picked up the screaming Gabriel and nursed him. Then she nursed the lightly fussing Jesse. As she diapered Jesse, she tried once again to find some physical difference between the babies. She couldn't. Once again she appreciated her smart husband. Who else would have thought of the colored material on their ankles? Then she laughed as Gabriel let out a yell that caused her to replace Jesse in the cradle and give Gabe a second helping. No way could those two babies ever be mixed up. Neither she nor Tom ever looked at the material to identify them. Each baby told her who he was whenever he needed something.

After dinner that day someone pounded on the front door. "Hello, Miz Dorland," a harried-looking young man said. "My wife's sick and can't take care of our younguns right now. Mrs. Gump said you wouldn't mind watching 'em since you got so many of your own anyways."

Rachel thought of the big washing she had to do that afternoon and the short nap she'd been hoping for. "I'm not sure," she said. "I have a big pile of work I have to do this afternoon. Couldn't Mrs. Gump watch them for you?"

The man shook his shaggy head. "She volunteers most of her time to the church so she can't. Could I get the children now? I have to get out to the job or there won't be nothing to feed my family this here winter."

Inasmuch as you have done it for the least of these, you've done it for Me. Rachel felt overwhelmed. But she'd do it for God. He'd help her. "Sure, bring them over," she said with a smile. "I'll watch them."

Fifteen minutes later he banged on the door again. When

Rachel opened it, three small children looked up at her with worried eyes. The man held a baby in his arms. He pushed the baby toward her, then shoved the others through the door. "I be thankin' ya," he said, running down the front steps.

The baby in her arms stared at her for a moment, looked toward the now closed door, opened up its mouth, and let out a bellow that would rival Tommy's best. Rachel looked at the other three. The little girl looked about three. One boy may have been about five and the other somewhere around two. The squalling baby seemed to be about Tommy's age, and Rachel had no idea whether it was a boy or girl. Then she noticed she didn't have a single change of clothing for anyone, not even a diaper.

The little girl pointed at the baby and jabbered something to Rachel, but Rachel couldn't understand a word. Rachel put the baby over her shoulder and started walking and patting its back. It cried even louder, and the smaller boy opened up his mouth and yelled louder than the baby.

Rachel felt positively terrified with four strange children, two of them shrieking, having no idea how to care for them. And her own three would be waking up soon, ready to claim her attention. On top of all that she had to do the washing or they'd run out of clothes.

"Can you tell me your name?" she finally asked the larger boy.

He shook his head no.

"Do you know your name?" she asked the little girl. The child nodded but didn't say anything.

"Tell me your name," Rachel said loudly to be heard over the two children's screams.

The little girl stuck her third and fourth fingers into her mouth and said nothing.

Rachel felt like running down the street after the children's father. If only Martha Lawford were here, together they could handle this mob of children. Then she remembered her best Friend. "Help me, Father," she said out loud. "I need help quick. I don't know what to do with these little ones and I have so many of my own. Oh, please help me, right now."

She'd barely gotten the words from her mouth when someone knocked on the door and it opened. "Oh, Papa," Rachel said, tears threatening. "God sent you before I asked. Thank You, God. Thank you, Papa. Someone just left these children with me and I don't know what to do with them."

"Get some bread," Papa said calmly, but loud enough to be heard over the racket.

Rachel, her head throbbing, ran after some bread and handed it to Papa, who handed it to the two crying children. They both took it, jammed it into their mouths, and stopped the noise.

Papa threw back his head and laughed. "What kind of a mess are you in now, Rachel?" he asked. "Let me guess. Mrs. Gump gave you some younguns to sew for so you'd have something to do."

Rachel felt a big lump in her throat as if she'd burst into tears any moment. But she couldn't do that. She simply couldn't. She swallowed, then swallowed again. "Some man brought them, Papa. I don't know who they are or even where they live."

"Well, let's get them something to eat. They're hungry."

Rachel gave the yelling baby to Papa and peeled some potatoes and onions for potato soup. When it was nearly finished, a huge yell from the bedroom announced Gabriel's desire to eat. Rachel turned terrified eyes to Papa. "You won't leave me, will you, Papa? Please?"

When he assured her he'd stay, she hurried to the bedroom but not in time to keep Gabriel from waking Tommy.

After carrying Tommy to Papa, she sat on the rocker in the bedroom and nursed the impatient baby. She hoped she could get the children fed before Jesse awakened. What she planned to do with them after they ate she had no idea. If they'd talk to her and tell her their names as well as where they lived, she wouldn't feel so terrified.

When Gabriel finished nursing, Rachel put him back into the cradle with Jesse, hoping he'd fall back to sleep. He didn't look tired, though.

She didn't even reach the stove before the baby's yells reached from the bedroom through the front room to the kitchen. She looked at Papa. "I don't know how to take care of so many children," she said.

Papa's blue eyes twinkled as though he were having the time of his life. "I'm holding this baby," he said. "Tommy's in his high chair waiting for his meal. Go get Gabriel, Rachel."

She did. Now how could she finish the soup with a baby in her arms? She took the big spoon and stirred the potatoes and onions. She could tell they were done. Still holding Gabriel, she poured a quart of cream into the soup. While that heated, she set the table with one hand. "Would you like to eat with them, Papa?" she asked.

"Sure. I didn't have any dinner." She was hungry too, but she wasn't foolish enough to think she'd get to eat with this mob to care for. Anyway, she'd just eaten dinner with Tom. Just eaten? It seemed weeks ago that she and Tom had sat at the table so quiet and peacefully.

After pouring small bowls of soup and slathering thick slices of homemade bread with butter, she put the children on chairs at the table. After looking at the smallest child a moment, she ran into the bedroom, put Gabriel in the middle of her bed, returned, and sat down with the unknown baby on her lap. "Would you pray, Papa? I'm not sure I have anything to be thankful for right now."

After Papa thanked God for the food and the children, Rachel put a spoon of soup to the baby's lips. It opened up its mouth and literally sucked the spoon in. When the soup was gone, it opened its mouth to yell again. Rachel quickly filled its mouth with another spoonful of creamy soup. She poked soup into the little mouth as quickly as it swallowed.

Meanwhile, Papa fed Tommy who gulped it down too. Rachel managed to help the others with bread and more soup. The next to youngest needed help spooning it into his mouth, so Rachel rotated feeding the two.

The soup ran out just when the children slowed down eating. Rachel finally had time to meet her father's eyes. "Did you get enough to eat, Papa?" she asked. "I forgot all about you."

He chuckled. "Am I a prophet? Those kids were starving, weren't they?"

Rachel nodded. They had been really hungry. And what would she have done without Papa? She grinned. She'd probably still be standing by the door wondering what to do.

About then she noticed the baby in her arms was soaking wet and smelling. In fact, everything the baby wore was drenched. She looked into its soiled face and heard herself thinking that she couldn't put one of her Tommy's clean diapers on it. And what about the other things? She'd been so careful with her babies' clothes. *Rachel, are you a respecter of persons?*

Well. The baby would wear Tommy's clothes. And she simply had to wash clothes. The babies would all be out of diapers before nightfall.

"Papa," she began, "could you watch the older three while I bathe and dress the baby? I guess I'll put some of Tommy's things on it."

Jesse let it be known that he'd been overlooked at feeding time so she fed him, then dipped warm water from the big reservoir on the stove into the wash tub. Holding the baby stranger on her arm, she washed the thin dirty hair, then the incredibly dirty little face. The baby didn't utter a sound while she ministered to it. Then she took off its wet clothes—it was another boy—and put him into the water.

He smiled and moved his legs in the water. "I'll bet that feels good, little man," Rachel said. She took the soap bar and scrubbed his body from top to bottom, then rinsed him off. Lifting him in an old towel, she dried him briskly and dressed him—dressed him in Tommy's clothes. He seemed to be just a tiny bit shorter and a lot thinner than Tommy. The baby smiled and cooed at Rachel now, seeming to have accepted her thoroughly. She took him in her arms and turned to Papa. "What now?" she asked.

Papa grinned again and motioned to the youngest in his charge. "At least one more needs clean clothes," he said. "That one stinks."

Rachel looked—and sniffed—and nodded. "But Papa," she wailed, "I don't have any bigger clothes."

"You can use two diapers on him."

Rachel changed the little boy, using two of Tommy's fluffy white diapers. In fact, the last two diapers. The little boy's other clothes were filthy and wet too, but she couldn't help that right now. She had to wash this very minute. Tommy wasn't used to being left wet and he wouldn't like it.

After carrying the tub outside and emptying it, she dipped it full of warm water and got the washboard. She managed to get most of the twins' diapers washed before both tiny babies began to fuss, Gabriel loudly and Jesse in his soft, patient voice. The rest of the babies' clothes weren't very dirty. Maybe she could let them fuss while she finished their things. But Gabriel knew how to get her every time by yelling louder than the competition.

"You can't be hungry already," Rachel cooed to her sweet-smelling, clean little boy. But he was. He proved it to her. When he finished, she nursed Jesse. Then she laid them in the cradle face to face. She'd discovered being able to see each other entertained them both. When they learned to use their hands she'd have to separate them so they wouldn't scratch each other.

Back to her washing. She scrubbed the rest of the baby clothes, then put in Tommy's. His took another hour. She checked the clock and decided the man would be back for his children soon, probably before she fixed supper. Tommy and the other little boy sat and looked at each other across the room. Content to watch each other, they made good nannies for one another.

The other children had sort of adopted Papa. Two had climbed into his lap and the other leaned against him. "Want to go outside and play hide and seek?" he asked.

No one answered or responded in any way.

When Tom came home he looked as if he'd walked into the wrong place. "Who's here?" he asked Rachel quietly.

She straightened from the wash tub and smiled into his eyes and shrugged. "I have no idea," she said. "Some man brought them for me to watch. Said his wife's sick." She giggled. "He also said Mrs. Gump told him I'd be glad to watch them because I already have so many. I guess that means I won't notice four more."

Tom looked puzzled a moment. "Well, you can't take care of all these little ones plus our own. Where do they live?"

Rachel swung her head back and forth, then stuck her hands back in the wash water. "I have no idea."

"What's their name?"

"Same song, second verse. Should get better but it's gonna get worse."

"Wait a minute. You don't know where they live and you

don't know their names. Do I have that right?"

She wagged her head up and down in an exaggerated fashion, scrubbed a flannel blanket, tossed it into the rinse tub, and reached for another. "That's about it. And in case you're curious, I don't know a single one of their first names either. One last fact, then you'll know everything I do. The two youngest are wearing our precious, clean, sweet-smelling Tommy's clothes." She giggled again and tossed another blanket into the rinse tub.

"Oh, there's one more thing," Nate said. "When I showed up here she was in tears and glued to the floor. If I hadn't come she'd still be standing there."

"Oh, Papa. Surely I'd have moved by now. Oh yes, Tom. I prayed to God for help and instantly Papa walked in. I bet he wishes I hadn't prayed."

"Oh no. I haven't had this much fun since the night the twins were born."

Tom wasn't laughing. "What if the man never comes back?"

five

Rachel sat down abruptly on a kitchen chair. "Not come back! Tom, he has to come back. His children are here."

"Why'd you let him leave them without getting his name?"

"Because he left before I knew what'd happened. Said he had to go to work and left. I forget where—or what he does." She thought a moment and gave up. "I have to get this washing finished, Tom, and make something for us all to eat—if the man doesn't come back first."

Tom pulled Rachel to him with a quick hug and kissed her soundly. "You do the washing. I'll find something for supper." He grinned at his father-in-law. "And Father Butler makes a wonderful nanny."

Rachel began scrubbing clothes on the board again, Papa watched babies, and Tom searched for something to eat. "Can I throw some potatoes into the oven?" he asked. Then he chuckled. "I mean all the potatoes."

"Whatever you want. If you're willing to cook it, I'm willing to eat it."

Tom began clanging things around in the kitchen and announced supper before Rachel finished washing.

Tom helped Nate wash up the children and put them around the table. Tommy sat in his high chair again and the smallest extra child sat on Rachel's lap, laughing and cooing. "He knows what we're about to do," Rachel said.

When Tom asked the Lord to bless the food, he also asked Him to bless the children's mother and help her get well quickly.

Tom held out a piece of butter-smeared bread to the oldest boy. "Want a piece of bread?" he asked. The boy nodded and reached for the bread. Tom held it back. "What's your name?" he asked in a soft, caring voice.

The boy hung his head and said nothing. Tom turned to the little girl. "Hi, honey," he said. "Would you like some bread?" She nodded. "Can you tell me your name first?" he asked. She shook her head no.

Tom turned to the next smaller one. "I'll bet you can't talk yet, can you?" he asked. The little boy nodded his head up and down. "What's your name?" he asked the child.

The little boy smiled all over his face and said something Rachel couldn't understand. Tom looked at her with raised eyebrows. She shrugged.

"What did you say?" he asked the small child. "Can you say it again?"

The boy said something. Again Rachel didn't understand.

A flash of brilliance shone in Tom's eyes. He turned to the oldest boy. "Do you know what your brother said?" The boy nodded. Tom grinned and gave him a hug. "Well, come on and tell me."

He hung his head and said nothing. Tom looked at Rachel, grinned, and shrugged. "Never hurts to try," he said. He got busy preparing baked potatoes in his plate, then transferring them to each child's. He put some cooked carrot onto each plate, a turnip, a piece of meat he'd cut into tiny pieces, and a half slice of bread spread thickly with butter. A glass of milk stood by each place.

Nate helped Tommy eat, Rachel fed the baby in her lap and also the little boy beside her. Tom kept refilling plates and buttering bread. All the children ate as if it were their first meal ever.

"I'll bet they haven't had anything to eat today," Tom said amazed.

Nate laughed. "Don't bet too much."

"We fed them potato soup for lunch," Rachel said. "And they ate just like this."

As the meal progressed Rachel felt not quite so frenzied, as if they might possibly live through the ordeal. Then Gabriel blew his horn from the bedroom, loud and clear. Rachel looked at the baby in her arms and the small child beside her, both their mouths open for the next bite.

Tom looked too and got up, returning a few minutes later with the baby. "I changed him but I can't do any more," he said. "We'll have to trade." When Rachel handed the baby visitor to Tom, he opened his mouth wide and a sound so loud came out that they couldn't even hear Gabriel.

As Rachel finished nursing Gabriel and put him back in bed with Jesse, it came to her that her two tiny babies had been unusually good that day. Come to think of it, Tommy had too. "Thank You, God," she said aloud. "You're always there when I need You. This day could have been a lot worse. Come to think about it, it wasn't all that bad. Thank You again, Father. I love You!"

After the meal ended, Rachel finished the washing and hung it on the line. Then she washed up the dishes. Almost all the dishes they owned. Papa and Tom played with Tommy and the other children. Rachel found all of them on the floor, rolling around on the rug, laughing and acting as if they were having a great time.

The clock on the table said seven o'clock. What if Tom was right? What if the man didn't come back after his children? What do you do when someone abandons his children with you?

Papa stood up. "I have to get back home," he said. "I just dropped by to see how Rachel's doing."

"No you didn't," Rachel said. "God sent you to help me. And it didn't turn out so badly, did it? If you hadn't come I'd have never lived through the afternoon. Who knows what would have happened to my own three babies. I just say, thank You, God. You knew who could handle the situation. And thank you, Papa. I pray their mama will be well and they'll be with her the next time you come."

"What do we do now?" Tom asked after Nate left. "Do we wait for their father—or do we start making beds on the floor?"

"I'm not sure we have enough blankets," Rachel said. "But I'm so tired I need to go to bed badly."

An hour later Rachel and Tom pulled out all the bedding they could find and made one big bed on the floor. They put the smallest child into bed with Tommy. Neither awakened as Rachel tucked them in together. Then they put the other three in the floor bed.

The youngest puckered up his face and opened his mouth. Rachel dropped to the bed beside him. "I'm going to lie right here with you for a while," she said softly, hugging the little boy to her. The child cuddled close to her and all three fell asleep in a few minutes.

"I hope Gabriel will sleep well tonight," Rachel told Tom as they crawled into bed. "I'm sure I've never been this tired in my whole life."

But Gabriel awakened in forty-five minutes, thinking he'd been neglected somehow. His forgiving smile reached the depth of Rachel's heart. When, however, he woke up every half hour the rest of the night his happy smiles didn't touch her quite so much.

The next morning Rachel could hardly wake up to face the new day. And she dreaded it even more when she remembered her extra four children—and Papa had gone home. How could she possibly care for all of them?

"I'll tell you what I'm going to do," Tom said as they ate breakfast alone—a lovely treat. "I'm going to go tell Mrs. Gump to come and get those youngsters. No one can expect you to take care of seven tiny children—really all babies."

Rachel giggled in spite of her fears. "She'll never do that, Tom. She's too smart. Tell me, why am I so dumb? And do you think the man will ever come back for them?"

"First off," Tom answered, "you aren't dumb. You just aren't used to people taking advantage of you. And no, I'm afraid the man won't be back."

Rachel felt like screaming. "What are we going to do then?" she asked quietly. "I don't know how I can handle all these children for even one more day, let alone forever."

"I'll go see Mrs. Gump and report back to you. All right?"

Rachel nodded.

Tom hadn't been gone long at all when the house erupted in children. Rachel hurriedly cooked some oatmeal with dried apples and cinnamon. She poured milk and made toast and buttered it. Then she set the children at the table and she held the baby. Tommy sat beside her in his high chair, banging a spoon on his tray. She poured oatmeal into small dishes, poured lots of milk into each one, and gave each child a spoon. The children acted once more as if this were their first meal in weeks. They each ate two bowls of oatmeal, a thick slice of buttered homemade bread, and a glass of milk. Rachel spooned cereal into Tommy's, the two-year-old's, and the other baby's mouths as fast as she could spoon. Most of the mouths were open all the time.

Tom stepped through the door before she finished feeding the bunch. "Hey, you've got it all figured out now," he said. "You're doing fine."

"What did she say, Tom?" Rachel said. "Tell me quick."

Tom laughed. "She said just what you said she would. She's too busy doing church work, she has too much running around to do, she's too old to handle small children, her house is too small. Want me to go on? I'm sure she had more reasons than that." He waved a small, brown package he held in his hands. "But I got some clothes out of her. Probably some you made. I told her if she didn't give me the clothes she'd have the children on her doorstep in thirty minutes."

Rachel felt as if she'd been hit with a shovel. "But Tom, we can't keep four extra children. I'm nearly dead after one day." She started to cry, but swiped away the tears with her hand.

He took her into his arms. "I'll run through my rounds today," he said. "I don't have any emergencies so I'll just tell each one I can't stop. Then I'll come home and help. How's that?"

Rachel nodded. "Better. But what about tomorrow? And the next day? And the next?"

He smoothed her hair away from her face and kissed her forehead. "Let's not worry about tomorrow. What does the Good Book say? Something about don't worry about tomorrow as each day has enough trouble of its own?"

Rachel laughed through her tears. "That sounds like us. Thanks for helping, Tom. I love you more than you can ever know."

Rachel always bathed her three babies right after breakfast. She stood looking down at the extra four. They needed baths worse than her own. Sighing, she pulled the wash tub from the nail where it hung. She'd put two in at once.

After dipping water, she grabbed the oldest boy, pulled off his clothes, and plopped him into the tub, then did the same for the little girl. The children loved the water, so Rachel scrubbed them thoroughly, including their hair. After drying them, she looked into the package Tom had brought home. She found two changes of clothes in almost the right sizes for each of the children. How had that ever happened? *Tom must have picked the clothes!* She hurriedly put the new clothes on the children and gently combed their hair. "How do you like that?" she asked, looking from the boy to the little girl.

The boy jerked his head up and down enthusiastically, his little hand running all over the new clothes. "I wike it," the little girl said.

"Oh!" Rachel said. "You can talk." She gave the girl a hug. "What's your name, honey?" she asked, still holding the child tightly.

"Bonnie," the little girl said. She leaned her head against Rachel, then looked into her eyes. "I wuv you," she added shyly.

"I love you too," Rachel said, surprising herself. She really did feel something special inside for the darling little girl. *Bonnie.*

Then Rachel remembered the rest of the family. After adding more warm water to the tub, she undressed the two smaller boys and put them in. She and the older boy both laughed as the baby slapped the water. Rachel scrubbed them thoroughly but quickly and washed their hair which was easy as neither had much. As she dried them she hoped desperately that Tom had found clothes for them too. When she checked the package again she found he had. She also found two pairs of pajamas for each of them.

The two-year-old laughed and touched his new clothes when Rachel dressed him, but she couldn't get him to say anything. When she had them all dressed and combed, she set them on the floor and looked at the tub. Shaking her head, she dipped the water from the heavy tub and carried it out. She would not put her precious little boys into that filthy water.

After another half hour her own boys were all clean and the little ones nursed. Knowing she wouldn't be able to do anything other than watch children, she put Gabriel and Jesse on blankets on the floor so they could watch the bigger children.

Strange, Rachel thought. *All these people milling around and no one to talk to.* She tried to talk to each of the three older ones, but Bonnie alone responded to her. Almost right away, Bonnie climbed into Rachel's lap and reached her thin little arms around her neck. "I wuv you," she said again.

Rachel hugged her close. "Do you know you're a beautiful little girl?" she asked. Bonnie shook her head but smiled her appreciation. "What's your big brother's name?" Rachel asked, still hugging Bonnie.

Bonnie pointed at the biggest boy. "Him Westa," she said.

"Westa?" Rachel said. She'd never heard the name, but there were probably several names in the world she hadn't heard.

Bonnie screamed with laughter. "Nooo," she yelled. "Westa."

It sounded the same to Rachel. "Westa?" she said again.

"No, Westa!" Bonnie yelled.

"Lester," the boy finally said. "She don't know how to talk."

Rachel gave Bonnie a pat on the cheek and smoothed her hair back, then smiled broadly at Lester. "Thank you, Lester. You talk just fine. Can you tell me your little brothers' names?"

He looked at the two-year-old and opened his mouth. Then he shut it without saying anything. His eyes moved to the baby but still he said nothing.

"I need to know what to call them," Rachel pleaded softly.

Bonnie pointed at the baby. "Dat Eddie," she yelled at the top of her voice. Her finger moved toward the two-year-old.

But before she said anymore the oldest boy supplied the name. "Willie. He's Willie."

"Well, thank you!" Rachel said. "Now I know all of you." She pointed at the oldest. "You're Lester." Her finger pointed at Bonnie in her lap. "Bonnie's right here in my lap." She squeezed Bonnie twice and let her finger move down to the two-year-old. "Willie's a big boy and there's Eddie over there by Tommy."

Bonnie leaned back and looked into Rachel's eyes. "Who you baby name?"

Rachel hugged Bonnie. "They're Gabriel and Jesse," she said.

"Get them," Bonnie ordered.

Just then Tom came into the room. "I'm all yours," he said. "What shall I do first?"

Rachel shook her head. She felt so overwhelmed she had no idea what to do. She'd have to wash clothes this afternoon but it was a little too soon now. "I don't even remember what I do around here." Then she remembered Bonnie. "But I learned the children's names," she said, pulling Bonnie to her. "Tom, this is Bonnie. And over here is her big brother Lester." Her finger moved toward the next one. "This is Willie and the little one's Eddie. Aren't those fine names?"

Tom squatted to the floor. "Those are great names. And don't they look beautiful in their new clothes? Did you find out how old these people are?"

Rachel leaned away from Bonnie. "No, can you tell me how old you are?"

"Free," Bonnie yelled. Rachel had never yet heard the little girl speak in a normal voice.

"All right!" Tom said. He turned to the oldest boy. "How old are you, Lester?"

He wouldn't answer but held up all the fingers on one hand and one on the other.

"You're six?" Tom asked. Lester nodded. "You're a nice big boy," Tom said. "What about the other two?"

No one seemed to know how old they were.

Rachel noticed a smell, so she changed four diapers. She grinned. At this rate it wouldn't take long before the diapers were all dirty and she could do the washing.

After a little while Tom offered to fix dinner while Rachel watched the children. Rachel managed to nurse the babies and put them into the cradle for a nap before Tom had dinner ready.

When Rachel washed up the children and put them at the table, she noticed Tom had fixed griddle cakes with maple syrup, eggs, and ham. *For dinner? Oh well, it looked good.* Tom prayed, thanking God for all their many blessings, including their large family. Rachel glared at him but he didn't notice.

When they finished and washed up the children, they played in the front room while Rachel cleaned up the kitchen and washed the dishes. Tom sneaked out to the kitchen and kissed her. "You're a good sport," he said.

Rachel grinned. "I didn't realize I had a choice."

He nodded. "Oh yes. Lots of women would have told me to get them out of here after the first night."

"But you aren't the one who let them come."

Just then someone knocked on the front door. Tom answered and Rachel followed.

The man who'd brought the children stood there, dripping from the pouring rain, looking dirty, torn, and bleak.

"Hello," Rachel said. "Tom, this is the children's father."

"Oh—" Tom said. "Kind of forgot to come after them, didn't you?"

The man looked surprised. "Came as quick as I could," he said. "My wife just died an hour ago."

six

Rachel felt her breath leave when the man said his wife had died. *Now what?* She couldn't possibly handle four more children. Yet how could she let them go back to a life worse than they'd had before?

"I'm terribly sorry to hear that, sir," she heard Tom say. *Thank God Tom was here.* Tom invited the man in and they all sat down together.

When the man first appeared, the children looked frightened, but they soon settled back to their playing.

After a long moment of silence, Tom spoke again. "Do you mind telling me what happened to your wife?"

The man ducked his head a moment as if he couldn't or wouldn't answer. Finally he raised his head and met Tom's gaze. "No, sir, I don't mind tellin' you, but I don't rightly know. She got sick about a month ago and just kept gettin' worse." He stopped and swallowed twice. "And now she died," he finally mumbled.

Tom looked troubled. "I'm sorry to bother you, sir, but did you have a doctor attending your wife?"

The man nodded. "Yessir. Dr. Ernest Miller. A fine man. Came 'most ever' day for a month, he did." He leaned his forehead on his hands, his elbows resting on his knees. Rachel's heart ached for the man's pain.

"May I ask what he did for your wife?" Tom asked. Rachel almost groaned. *Why couldn't Tom stop with the questions and just tell the man he was sorry?* All this talk had to hurt the man.

"It's all right," the man said. His voice sounded as if he

should clear his throat. He closed his eyes and thought a moment before continuing. "I guess the first thing he did was give her something to make her puke and have a bad case of the runs." He shook his head. "After he done that she couldn't hardly take care of the young'ns anymore. She didn't seem to get better so he had to bleed her. She still didn't get better so he bled her again. That time he took a lot of blood." He put his head in his hands again and his shoulders shook. "He took a lot," he finally mumbled. "It shoulda helped."

"What then?" Tom asked after waiting a long time. "I guess she still didn't improve."

"Do you really need to do this?" Rachel asked softly.

Tom nodded. "I'm sorry to hurt you, sir, but it's important that I ask these questions. Do you remember what happened next?"

"Yes. She never got out of bed after that. I left Lester to care for the little tykes but they cried all the time. It bothered Ruth a lot. But I had to work or I'd lose my job. Well, a couple of days later he gave her the stuff that made her throw up and have the trots again—I think he called it diree. She was real sick by this time. I figgered it was too late, but the doctor still thought he could save her. He took blood three more times but nothing seemed to help." His voice faded away. He hiccupped twice and his shoulders shook some more.

"Was that when you brought the children here?" Tom asked, his voice almost a whisper.

"I brought them here when she didn't wake up no more. The doctor still said she'd get better, but I lost hope. I didn't want them there alone with her when—you know. So I went to the Ladies' Aid, then brought 'em over here."

"Did he do anything for her after you brought the children here? In the last day or two?"

The man nodded, his face in his hands. After a moment he

cleared his throat and looked into Tom's eyes again. "He bled her once more." The man didn't say anything more for several minutes. The children stopped and watched their father a moment, then went back to their play. When the man looked at Tom again, he shrugged. "I don't know what happened, but you can see the doctor tried everthin' he knew."

Tom shook his head sadly. "Yes," he said with a catch in his voice. "He certainly did."

Rachel's heart nearly stopped, fearing Tom would say something about the treatment being wrong. But he didn't.

"What are you going to do now?" he quietly asked the man. "By the way, sir, we still don't know your name."

"Max Barer."

Tom jumped to his feet and extended his hand. "Tom Dorland here and my wife, Rachel." The men shook hands.

"Now," Tom said kindly, "I suppose you haven't had time to decide anything yet."

"Well, I bin thinkin a lot." He stopped and swallowed hard. "The thing is—I don't know what to do with the younguns." His eyes reddened even more. "It ain't that I don't like my children, but I don't make enough money to hire a nanny. I cain't stay home with my tykes or I ain't got money to feed 'em."

Tom got up and gripped the man's shoulder a moment. "I understand, Max. I wish I had some good advice, but I don't. My wife is always willing to help anyone, but we have three children ourselves and the oldest just turned one. You can see she's more than busy already. I took off work today to help her because there's no way she can take care of yours and ours alone. She has to do a big washing every day, and the truth is when she has seven tiny ones to care for she can't do anything except care for them. I've been cooking and her father's been helping too."

Max nodded. "I know. It ain't yer problem." He got up.

"Come on, Lester. Grab them tykes and let's go."

The three oldest Barer children looked up and saw their father preparing to leave, planning to take them with him. Lester looked unhappy, and Bonnie and Willie opened their mouths wide and bawled as loud as possible.

"Here. You stop that," Max said. "We have to go home now."

"I want to stay here," Lester whined. "I like it here."

"Me too," Bonnie echoed. "Me too."

"It don't matter!" Max roared. "We got to get on home."

The middle two bellowed even louder, Lester joined in, and baby Eddie began crying too. Then Tommy joined the chorus and wailed as loudly as any of them. Rachel quickly snatched him into her arms and sat back down, stroking his back, his arms, and his legs. He quieted and cuddled against her.

Rachel looked at Tom and he looked at her. She didn't want to let them go, but Tom was right. She couldn't care for all of them alone. And both Tom and Papa had to work, just as Max Barer did.

Tom moved beside Max. "Let me help you get the children home," he said. "Then we'll know where you live in case we think of something."

Tom carried Willie and held Bonnie's hand while Max carried Eddie. A few minutes later Rachel heaved a big sigh and shut the door. Oh my! She'd never heard such a quiet room. "What have we done, God?" she burst out. "What will happen to those dear children now? I'd have kept them for awhile, Father, except I can't do it alone. And I can't ask Papa and Tom to help all the time. They have their own work to do. Oh, Father, show us what You'd have us do."

Rachel wandered through the house carrying Tommy, not enjoying the quiet at all. She had a strong feeling that she'd done something awful. Gabriel's call brought her mind back to reality so she went after him. She took him into the front room, carefully put Tommy on the floor beside her, and nursed the hungry baby. She'd barely finished with Gabriel when Jesse started snuffling in the cradle. She finished feeding Jesse as Tom walked in.

"Well," he said cheerfully, dropping onto the settle, "the Barers live only about a half mile from here, over by the dairy." Tommy saw his papa sit down, crawled to him, and pulled himself up to his knee. Tom lifted the baby into his arms.

Rachel held Jesse over her shoulder to burp him. "What's going to happen to those children?" she asked.

Tom shook his head. "I have no idea. I'm afraid Max is so distraught he won't even remember to feed them. And I suspect they'll be alone while he's at work." He shook his head. "Sad story."

"It's awful, Tom. I wish I could help. I really do. I know the thought of caring for them scared me to death, but now I feel responsible."

Tom pulled her onto his lap beside Tommy. "Do you think you could take care of all the little ones for a while if I hurried home every day and helped you? You wouldn't have to do anything but watch children while I'm gone."

"Yes, Tom, I want to. I've been trying to figure how I could care for them without involving you and Papa."

"You realize they'll be filthy again the next time you see them? In fact every time you see them."

"I'll give them a bath every morning. They like that. I'll do all right, Tom, if I just know I don't have to do anything but take care of them until you come home. Maybe we should take them completely."

Tom kissed her neck. "We don't know that he'd let us, love. Besides, he needs the children to give him a reason for living. Even though they make it hard for him right now, they're also keeping his mind busy."

Tom walked back to the Barer place to see what Max thought about their plan. Rachel wished she could have gone, but they hadn't figured out how to carry three babies a distance yet. While he was gone she started the washing but was soon interrupted by a visitor, Mrs. Gump.

"I see you don't have the Barer children anymore," she said.

"I'm going to have them every day while their father works," Rachel said. "But they're gone right now."

"Well," Mrs. Gump said, "I've come to talk about Mrs. Barer's funeral. Could you cook a meal for afterwards if we bring you the food?"

"I don't think so, Mrs. Gump. I'll probably be taking care of the Barer children and with seven small children and babies I don't dare take on anything else."

"Oh, the children will be at the funeral. You can cook the meal while everyone's at the church."

If you do it for the least of these, Rachel. Maybe she should wait and talk to Tom. No, she'd better do it for God. She nodded. "All right. Be sure to bring me the food early on so I can get it finished in time. I still have my own three little babies, you know."

"I'll be sure it gets to you in plenty of time. Thank you, Rachel. You're an angel." The woman walked down the wooden sidewalk as if she might take off flying any time.

"I'll bet she got stuck with the job," Tom said when she told him. "No wonder she felt happy when she palmed it off on you." He kissed her nose. "You're an easy touch, you know."

"I know. What did Max say about leaving the children here?"

"Oh! He accepted gratefully. I've never felt so sorry for anyone, Rachel, as I do that man. He's so crushed he's debilitated." He picked up Tommy and sat down beside the table. "Know what makes me so upset?" he asked. "The woman probably had only some minor ailment until that doctor got hold of her. The doctors are killing their patients, Rachel! And it has to stop!"

"What can one man do, Tom? And are you sure you're right? After all, the medical schools teach exactly what the man did."

"I know. But the schools in Europe have it figured out and are trying their best to get our medics straightened out. They won't listen. She died, Rachel, not from her illness, but from that stuff they did to her. Didn't you know that's why I asked all those questions?"

Rachel nodded. "I knew. I was terrified you'd tell Max what you thought and he didn't need to hear that right now. He might have gone back and killed the doctor. And the doctor did exactly what he'd been taught to do."

Tom slumped down over Tommy. "I wish I'd been taking care of her. Things might be a whole lot different."

"You don't know that, Tom."

His red-rimmed eyes met hers. "I guess I don't, but it couldn't have turned out worse."

She had to agree. She went back to her washing and Tom started supper again. She smiled. This could get to be a habit. Probably would in fact.

❧

The next morning Rachel hurried through her work so she'd have time to cook the meal for the Ladies' Aid. When she had everything finished that she'd planned to do before she cooked the meal, the food hadn't arrived yet. She paced the house waiting. She didn't want to start doing anything because she'd have to put it away when the food came. She sat down at the piano and played one song after another while she waited.

It still hadn't arrived when Tom came home for dinner. Rachel fed him and Tommy roast venison sandwiches and dried pea soup. Still the food hadn't come.

"Do you think someone else is cooking it?" she asked Tom. "Or will they bring it to me when it's too late to cook it?"

That's what happened. Mrs. Gump hurried up the sidewalk an hour after Tom went back to work. "Sorry, I'm late," she puffed. "Fortunately it's all quick-cooking items."

When the woman left, Rachel looked through the box. Potatoes, rice, parsnips, turnips, dried peas, carrots. That was it. Nothing to drink, no bread and butter, and no meat.

After looking through the things again, Rachel decided it would have to be soup. She had enough meat and onions for soup, two loaves of bread, and plenty of butter. As she began preparing the vegetables, Tommy insisted on being held. She held him on one arm while she tried to peel potatoes, but it went slow as she had to be careful not to cut his inquisitive little hands. She tried to put the little boy down a few times but he objected strenuously. Then Gabriel's bellow brought everything to a standstill while she nursed him. As she changed him she noticed by the clock the funeral had already begun. She'd never have the food ready in time. She hurried Gabriel back to bed and rushed to the kitchen.

As she peeled the vegetables, Tommy fussed and held out his arms. "I'm sorry, babe, but I can't," she kept telling him, feeling frustrated not to have the food ready and guilty not to be able to cuddle her baby. Finally Tommy gave up and fell asleep at her feet. Scooping him into her arms she carried him into the bedroom and gently laid him in his bed.

Twenty minutes later the soup bubbled on the stove. She hoped against hope it would be cooked by the time someone came after it.

Forty-five minutes later Rachel tasted the soup. *Mmmmm.*

Perfect and cooked to a turn. But no one came after the soup. She shook her head. Some people just weren't reliable.

Gabriel soon yelled that he was hungry, followed by the quiet little sounds of Jesse. Rachel nursed Gabriel and put him back down. Someone knocked on the front door. Rachel put her clothing back together and answered the door.

She couldn't believe her eyes when a dozen people walked up her sidewalk, and many carriages approached the house from the direction of the church. Surely Mrs. Gump wouldn't have told people to come here without telling her.

"Are we too early?" the woman at the door wanted to know. What could Rachel do? She didn't have half enough dishes or silverware, not to mention a place for people to sit and eat.

Rachel tried a tremulous smile. "You're not too early, Mrs. Greenwillow, but I think you came to the wrong place."

The woman glanced down the sidewalk at the people, then the road filled with carriages, and shook her head. "The minister announced the meal would be here right away."

Just then the Barer family arrived and the three older children all threw themselves into her arms. "Can we live with you?" "Don't make us go away anymore," and "I wuv you, I wuv you, I wuv you," came into her ears at once. Rachel's brain began to spin. *How do you tell three motherless children to get out of your way so you can figure out how to feed thirty people? So many people you have no idea how to go about the task. When you have only half enough food anyway.*

seven

"How you doing, love?" a soft voice said into her ear as strong arms enveloped her. "Looks like we're it for serving the meal, right?"

Rachel eased Willie to the floor and patted Bonnie and Lester. Then she threw herself into Tom's arms. "What are we going to do?" she asked, feeling wild tears about to erupt. "They didn't bring nearly enough food and we don't have enough dishes or silver. Or even a big enough table. Tom, what can we do?"

"Don't make me go away!" "Feed me first. I'm hungry," Bonnie and Lester pleaded loudly.

"First off," he said with a calm smile, "let's don't panic." He squatted down to talk to the children. "Could you go into the bedroom and find Tommy's blocks?" he asked quietly. "You can play with them in there if you like. Right now, Rachel is going to be real busy. Could you do that for her?" He stood up and the children followed Lester into the bedroom.

Rachel looked up at Tom and shook her head. "I saw you do that but I don't believe it." Then her predicament rushed back into her mind. People stood shoulder to shoulder in the large front room. And a few more carriages still pulled up and stopped.

"Why don't we feed as many as we can, wash the dishes, and feed more?"

Rachel shook her red head wildly. "That would take all afternoon. Let's serve soup in plates, mugs, bowls, whatever we can find. We'll give each person a fork or spoon

71

but not both. And one slice of buttered bread. By the time the dishes are used up the soup will be gone too."

Tom agreed. "We'll let them take their meal outside and eat it standing up. We're lucky the sun's shining. It isn't very warm but at least it's decent for late October." He turned to the people. "We didn't realize we were serving this meal," he said cheerfully, "but we'll do our best until the food runs out. Let's bow our heads in prayer."

After Tom prayed, asking God to especially bless Max Barer and his children, he started a line and handed out whatever he could find to put soup in. Rachel dipped soup with a dipper, giving each person one and a half dips. When she'd filled eighteen dishes with soup, Gabriel yelled for his meal.

"I'll dip soup," Tom said, taking the dipper. Rachel thought she couldn't sit still long enough for Gabriel to finish, and Jesse awakened too. Rachel suddenly realized Jesse had missed a nursing again. Not too unusual, but she tried to prevent it. After nursing Jesse and changing all three babies, she hurried back to the kitchen.

"Still going," Tom said. "We may be able to serve everyone a small meal."

The soup gave out with just a half-dozen people left, besides Rachel and Tom and the Barer children. "What do we do now?" Rachel asked.

Tom grinned. "Got anything else?"

Rachel remembered the beans they'd had last night. She put them on the stove and soon Tom served them. "Could you make some biscuits?" he asked when the bread neared extinction. So she made a triple batch. She fixed some oatmeal cereal and poured maple syrup and cream over it. Tommy and the Barer children ate the cereal as if it were a great treat—and so did their guests. Rachel felt as if she were about to burst from tension. She'd never been in such a mess before in her life.

"Thanks for the treat," Mrs. Greenwillow said as she left. "I've been hearing what a fine cook you are, and now I know for myself."

"I wonder what she ate," Tom said, chuckling.

Rachel shook her head. "Who knows? At least they're all finishing and will be gone in a little while."

When the last guest left, Tom grabbed Rachel and twirled her around. "We did it!" he said joyfully. "Proves together we can do anything—with the Lord's help."

Rachel reluctantly began washing clothes. She'd never felt so tired in her life. At least not that she could remember.

❧

The next morning someone banged on the door before Rachel had pried her eyes open. As usual Gabriel had awakened her more times than she cared to remember. As usual Jesse and Tommy had slept through the night without awakening.

She elbowed Tom. "Honey, someone's at the door." He groaned and rolled over.

The banging began again. "Tom!" she said louder, "someone's knocking the door down."

That time Tom awakened, pulled on his pants, and ran to the front door. Rachel followed at a safe distance. *Probably Mrs. Gump,* she thought as Tom opened the door.

"Thought ye were gone already," Max Barer said. "Fer a minute I thought I'd have to take the younguns home again."

Tom rubbed his eyes. "We're here, Max, but we overslept."

"Well, if yore missus can keep the children, I'll be getting on to my job."

"All right. Good luck, Max."

Well, might as well get dressed and face the day. Gabriel would soon be screaming for his first meal. Maybe she could get the older ones fed first.

ða

Two days passed uneventfully. Busy, harried, but uneventful. But the third day, Rachel had just finished cleaning up the Barer children when she heard a quick knock on the door. Recognizing the knock she hurried to open the door to Mrs. Gump.

"I've been wanting to see you," Rachel said eagerly. "Come in."

The woman carried a large box in her arms. "I really can't stay," she said. "I just brought you some sewing to keep you out of mischief."

Rachel's heart slid into her shoes. She didn't have time for mischief—or sewing. "You have to find someone else to do your sewing," she said. "Caring for seven tiny children is an unending job."

Mrs. Gump shook her wiry gray head. "We're counting on you, Rachel. You knew you had this to do before you took on more children."

"But Mr. Barer had no place to leave his children," she said. "If I didn't care for them he'd have had to leave them alone."

"I'll just set the box down here," Mrs. Gump said in a honey-sweet voice. "You get at these things right away, hear? We never know when someone will need them." She started toward the door but Rachel interrupted.

"Wait a minute," she said. "I've been wanting to ask you something. Where were you after Mrs. Barer's funeral? You didn't tell me I had to do the whole thing alone."

"My dear, there was no need for both of us to spend our afternoon doing the same thing. One of us would have been wasting our time."

Rachel grinned. "I think we both could have found something to do. Did you think you brought enough food? They ate that and everything we had in the house too."

"Well, that's why we ask the doctor's wife. We know you can afford whatever it takes." She faced the door again and said over her shoulder, "Thank you, dear, for sewing the clothes."

As the door closed, Rachel glared at the box of material. "You can just sit there until you rot for all I care," she informed it.

She spent the rest of the day caring for and playing with the children. They all had a good time and Rachel didn't feel pressure. When Tom came home she did the washing and Tom started supper. Rachel got soaked hanging the clothes on the line in the pouring rain. It looked as if she'd have to start hanging the clothes in the house—what a mess with all the children. Tom had supper nearly ready when Max Barer came after his children.

When they saw him, they all started crying together as if it had been planned. Rachel knew, though, that they were too young for that; instead, the first one started and they all followed the leader.

"Why don't you wash up a little and eat with us?" Tom asked the worn-looking man. "I cooked the meal and it looks as if I made plenty."

The man gladly complied, washing himself and each of his children. Rachel fed Eddie, Tom fed Tommy, and Max helped Willie. One thing about the Barer children, they ate anything put before them.

Rachel and Tom kept the Barer children every day, and they fell into a schedule, exactly the same every day. Rachel did the washing while Tom fixed supper. Max ate with them, and the children put up a terrible fuss when he took them home.

Rachel managed to walk past the box of material for a few days, but as she got used to having all the children around she began to feel guilty for not fixing clothes for the "needy children." She pulled out the material and started working. If she made only a few seams each day it was something. Mrs. Gump kept coming and marching away with a straight back, showing her displeasure at Rachel's dawdling, as she called it.

One day Bonnie Barer lay around most of the day and cried every time something didn't go her way. At lunch time she wasn't hungry and slept most of the afternoon. Rachel felt her forehead. Hot. Really hot. Well, Tom would be home pretty soon.

When Tom came home he agreed Bonnie was sick. "Let's bathe her with cool water," he said. As they bathed the little girl, Tom fretted. "I hope Max doesn't call that bleeder."

Rachel didn't know what to think. Why would Tom know more about treating people than all the most up-to-date medical schools? What if he took charge of Bonnie and still she died? Then Rachel would think the other doctor should have been called. She shook her head. How was she supposed to know?

That evening when Rachel told Max that Bonnie was sick, he sighed as if this were just too much. "I suppose I'll have to call doc," he said. "Goin' to be many a year a'fore I get him paid for Ruth. Now I got to start over?"

"No!" Tom said quickly. "You don't, Max. Let me take care of Bonnie."

Max jerked around to face Tom. "You? You want to be a doctor and take care of my Bonnie?" He shook his head. "My Bonnie's goin' to have a real doctor, if'n I never get him paid."

Tom grinned. "I am a doctor, Max. A real one too. And I won't charge you a cent."

Max looked at Rachel with a big question mark in his eyes.

Rachel smiled. "He's a real doctor, Max. He takes care of sick people all day long every day."

Max still looked suspicious. "Where you learn to be a doctor?"

"In Illinois. I graduated from medical school just before I joined the wagon train that brought me out here. I guess you could say I started practicing on the wagon train. Rachel helped me. That's how we met."

Max dropped into a chair and thought awhile. Finally he raised his eyes to meet Tom's. "That's why you asked all them questions about Ruth, ain't it?"

Tom nodded. "Yes. I wanted to learn all I could about her illness."

Max seemed relieved. "Well, you just go to it then. I took a liking to both of you two. If you think you're experienced enough to handle whatever she has, you take care of her, Tom. Want me to leave her here tonight?"

Tom gladly accepted responsibility for Bonnie. As soon as Max left with the other children, Tom told Rachel what he wanted done for the little girl. "I want her to drink a cup of water every hour she's awake." He sat for awhile thinking. "Could we make a soup with vegetables and meat? We could chop it up fine and feed it to her often."

After Rachel nursed the babies, changed all three, and put them all on the floor, she and Tom made a big pot of soup, enough for everyone. They ate and fed Tommy.

Rachel laughed while they were eating. "Has it ever crossed your mind that when we have only our own family again, if we ever do, it will be hardly worth cooking or washing or doing anything, there will be so few of us?"

Tom nodded and joined her chuckle. "Strange, isn't it? There were so many of us until the Barers came along. Now it takes both families to make a lot of people."

Bonnie was a good patient and tried to do whatever Tom

asked her. "Try to keep her quiet," Tom said the next morning as he left. "I'm sure she's all right, but let's just keep her quiet for another day."

"Is Bonnie going to die?" Lester asked soon after Tom left.

"Good heavens, no!" Rachel said laughing. "Bonnie's going to be just fine."

Lester nodded and dropped to the floor to play.

That evening, Dr. Miller dropped by. "I heard through the grapevine that Bonnie Barer is sick. I just thought I'd have a look at her," he said.

Rachel closed her eyes and thanked God Tom was there.

"Sure," Tom said. "Come right on in." He led the doctor to Bonnie's bed. "She's not very sick," he said. "Just some little childhood thing."

The doctor looked her over. "I'm not so sure," he told Tom. "I think we better give her some tartar emetic or at least some calomel."

Tom shook his head almost violently. "Not while I'm in charge. She's doing just fine."

"She still has a fever," Dr. Miller said. "Obviously she has far too much vitality and it'll get her if we don't get it."

"I don't agree," Tom said. "You'll have to take her from my care before you do anything like that."

The doctor moved toward the door. "I'm sure that can be arranged, Mr. Dorland." He closed the door behind him as he left.

Max returned with the doctor within the hour. "I unnerstan' you two don't agree on Bonnie's treatment," he said.

"We strongly disagree," Tom said. "I love Bonnie, and I can't possibly allow anyone to treat her with that stuff."

"Why?"

Tom sucked on his lip as he thought. Rachel knew he was trying to decide how much to say and how to say it in order not to hurt Max any more than necessary. "Why?" he finally repeated softly. "Because it doesn't work. Not only that but it sucks the life right out of a person." His eyes sought Max's. "Don't let him do it, Max. You'll lose your little girl if he starts that."

"Who says?" Dr. Miller boomed. "Where did you go to medical school, Dorland?"

Tom grinned. "Right here in the United States, Miller. I'm ashamed to admit it but I did. This treatment is left over from the eighteenth century and it's time to dump it."

Dr. Miller shook his head. "Here we are arguing methods of treating illness while a little girl is growing worse by the minute."

Tom took a deep breath. "Max, is your little girl worse than when you left her with us?"

"She don't look worse to me. She's a-wantin' to get up and play now."

"Children always want to play," Dr. Miller said. "You can't tell a thing by that."

"How do you tell then?" Max wanted to know.

"By the fever—and other things."

"Her fever's way down," Tom said. "That's why she wants to play. Tell us how you know she's worse, doctor."

The doctor appeared uncomfortable. "There are ways, but I'm afraid neither of you would understand. I think I'll just go along if my services here are not needed."

"I dunno—" Max stammered.

Tom held his hand to the doctor. "Thanks for stopping," he said. "Feel free to stop again anytime."

"Are you real sure about this?" Max asked after the older doctor had gone.

Tom nodded. "Absolutely. Just relax and trust me."

Two days later Bonnie was up and playing as if she'd never been sick.

Things quieted down after Bonnie's recovery and Rachel finally finished the sewing. Mrs. Gump had stopped coming, and Rachel felt fearful to take the things back to her. For sure Mrs. Gump would bring Rachel another box of material. Still, the clothes were finished and someone might need them. So one morning she asked Tom to drop them off as he went by the church.

Sure enough, that afternoon Mrs. Gump came by with more material. "Don't be discouraged when it takes a long time," Rachel said. "I'm very busy."

The next day a young woman from the church, Wilma Johnson, came to see Rachel, bringing her two small children. Rachel helped the children, Alicia, four, and Richard, six, get acquainted with the Barer children, and stayed with them until they played together.

"You know my husband ran off and went back to Missouri, don't you?" the young woman asked Rachel.

Rachel felt horrified. *How could any man do that to the woman he'd promised to love forever?* "No! I didn't hear a thing."

Wilma nodded her head up and down, up and down. "Yes. That's exactly what he did. So here I sit with two children to support. How can I support two children when I have to take care of two children? Does that make sense, Rachel?"

"No. This horrible thing doesn't make sense at all."

"Well, I have a chance to work as a clerk at the General Mercantile. Mrs. Gump told me you'd be glad to watch my children as you have to stay home with your own anyway."

eight

Rachel felt her breath coming fast. Her pulse pumped in the top of her head. Her hands clenched at her sides, then unclenched and clenched again. She discovered her teeth gritting together. What right did Mrs. Gump have to do this to her? And why would she do it? The more children Rachel cared for the less time she had to sew for the Ladies' Aid. *Get hold of yourself, Rachel. This woman had nothing to do with it. She's not the one conspiring against you.*

Rachel took a long, deep breath and tried to smile. "I'm sure you saw my large family. I'm caring for seven children now," she said, "four of them one year old and younger. That's about my capacity. If I took your children, they wouldn't get the care they need. I'd—"

"Oh, they don't need much care," Wilma interrupted. "They're past all that baby stuff. They might even help you care for the babies."

Rachel gulped. She'd never let little children care for her babies. She shrugged. "I just don't think I could handle any more. I'm sorry, but that's how it is."

Wilma's big brown eyes looked desperate. "But they won't be any trouble. I promise they won't. I can even bring their dinner if that will help."

Inasmuch as you have done it for the least of these. . .but how could she take on more? She was only human. Well, at least she couldn't do it without talking to Tom first. It wouldn't be fair since he had to help with the Barer children already.

She shook her head. "If I hear of anyone who can help

81

I'll let you know right away, Wilma. I wish I could, but my husband has to help with the ones we have. He takes care of the children and makes supper while I do the washing every day. Why don't you drop back in a day or two? In the meantime I'll check around."

The young woman went away sad.

When Tom came home for dinner, Rachel told him about the young woman alone with two children. "I felt so sorry for her I almost took them on in spite of the load we already have," she added.

Tom shook his light brown head. "I don't know how you'd handle it, but maybe we should pray about it. If God says it's all right, I'll give it a try."

Rachel threw herself into his arms. "Did I ever mention that I love you, Tom Dorland? Well I do. But if we did this you'd probably have to cook supper for them too."

He grinned. "I always cook too much anyway. But if you do take the children, do it on a trial basis. It may be too much for you."

They got down on their knees right then with the children playing around them and asked their heavenly Father if He wanted them to take more children. They waited silently for awhile, their heads bowed, listening. After five minutes, Tom got up, took Rachel's hand, and helped her to her feet.

"Did He say anything to you?" she asked.

"Not yet. But He will. Just keep listening."

When Tom and Rachel went to bed that night, neither had felt God's answer. "He'll speak to one of us in the night," Rachel said. "Let's just keep listening."

Rachel awakened the next morning with an answer that she didn't understand. She didn't know whether she'd dreamed it, or if God had spoken while she slept, or if He'd just put the words in her heart.

"He said I have to learn to tell His voice from Satan's,"

she told Tom. "He said that Satan knows the Bible better than any human being and loves to quote it to people wrongly to discourage them. He doesn't care how he gets people discouraged. He'll do whatever will work. Just think, Satan knows the verse that's been plaguing me. Inasmuch as you have done it for the least of these, you've done it for Me." She looked at Tom and rolled her eyes. "How's a person supposed to know who's talking, Tom?"

"I guess we have to listen and use our brain. God probably expects us to know when we're full up with good deeds." He pulled her close to him. "Did He tell you what to do about the extra children?"

She shook her head. "I can't remember any more. Do you think this means we shouldn't take Wilma's kids? What're we going to do, let them starve?"

Tom released her and jumped out of bed. "That wouldn't be my advice, love. I don't recommend letting anyone starve, ever. But for now, let's get this day going before Max gets here with his brood."

Rachel and Tom, moving around in the room, awakened Gabriel who gave his mighty clarion call. Rachel scooped him into her arms before he woke Jesse and Tommy, but they both woke anyway before she finished with Gabriel. Tom took Tommy, and Rachel nursed Jesse, then hurried to the kitchen to make breakfast for the big brood of children.

As Rachel fed Eddie and helped Willie, she laughed. "Remember when I panicked at caring for all these children? Now it seems normal."

Rachel watched for Wilma all that day and the next, but she didn't come. As she cared for the children, she watched carefully to see if she had time for two more. Maybe Wilma was right; if her children were a little older they might be able to help Rachel. She grinned to herself. She was truly getting used to these seven. She was also getting used to having her eyes burn with the need for sleep and her muscles ache from tending so many babies. She just might make it with the extra two.

Two days later Wilma knocked on the front door and came in, her arms wrapped around herself. "Have you noticed how cold it is out there? More like December than November. Going to be a tough winter." Then she laughed. "I came on in because I knew you wouldn't have time to come to the door. Well, I don't have to ask if you found anyone to take care of my little ones. I've tried everyone I know and some I don't."

Rachel smiled. "I talked to Tom and we decided to give it a try. I don't know if I can handle it so it will just be a two-week test. Is that fair?"

Wilma squealed and hugged Rachel. "My children aren't any trouble. You'll see." She hugged Rachel again. "You don't know how this makes me feel. I was beginning to think I'd have to put my children into an orphanage so they wouldn't starve to death." She danced around the room. "I get to start working," she said to no one in particular. Then she turned back to Rachel. "May I bring them tomorrow? The merchant said I could start whenever I'm able. And we desperately need the money."

So the next morning found Rachel in charge of nine children. She tried to find things for them to play with, but with her children so much younger it was hard. She'd try to make a couple of rag dolls. Maybe the boys could bring some toys.

Rachel soon discovered whenever she turned her back, four-year-old Alicia Johnson pushed Tommy and Eddie down. Both little boys were just beginning to walk and it didn't take much to unbalance them. Both boys spent their morning crying, and Rachel spent her morning cuddling them and telling Alicia she mustn't do that.

The extra two children fit at the table just fine, and Rachel appreciated their ability to feed themselves.

When Tom left after dinner, Alicia put her energies to picking up the babies and carrying them around. Rachel couldn't let her do that because she'd drop one for sure. The babies may have been young, but they both knew they didn't like the way Alicia carried them and they let Rachel know.

By the time Tom came home to watch youngsters and prepare supper, Rachel felt she'd been through a tornado. How could she possibly do a big washing now? Washing the clothes the Barer children wore while at her house made the washing even larger.

"One thing I know now," Rachel told Tom, "is that watching all the children will get easier as we get used to it."

Rachel did the washing, telling herself she simply couldn't start doing Wilma's washing too. She couldn't.

Wilma came after her two before Rachel finished the washing, so her children didn't eat supper with them. Rachel wondered if she should have invited them to stay, then told herself she couldn't care for the entire world.

When Rachel fell into bed that night, every bone and muscle in her body ached. Her head ached too. She awakened early in the morning wondering what had happened during the night. "Did you put Gabriel in bed with me to nurse?" she asked Tom.

He shook his head. "I don't think so. Maybe he slept all night."

Rachel doubted that but didn't worry about it. Both of her babies were fat and healthy. Amazingly, Jesse stayed as fat as Gabriel, who nursed much oftener. Jesse weighed twelve pounds, six ounces, and Gabriel weighed twelve pounds, five ounces.

The next day Rachel didn't feel quite so exhausted before she did the washing. She'd get this bigger job conquered, too. She asked Tom to hang lines in the spare bedroom as the clothes weren't getting dry outside anymore—and there were simply too many people running around to hang them in the front room or kitchen.

One day Mrs. Gump dropped by. "I've been much too busy lately, but I finally made it after the clothes. You probably finished them so long ago you've forgotten about them."

"Wrong, Mrs. Gump," Rachel said. "I've made only one or two items and I doubt I'll be doing any more soon. Do you remember sending Wilma Johnson to me? Well, I'm caring for her children as well as Max Barer's. I'm sure you won't believe me, but caring for nine small children, four of them babies, keeps me busy."

"Well, just remember you had this commitment to me before you had any children, other than your own. Good day, Rachel." The tall, stringy woman rushed through the door and down the board sidewalk.

Rachel sat down to think about that woman who could wreck her peace of mind so easily. Immediately, Tommy wanted up and Eddie followed. She put them both on her lap, cuddling and patting them. "I'm never going to know what it's like to care for just my own little family, am I, baby?" she whispered to Tommy.

A few minutes later she put the babies down, feeling better. The sweet babies had helped Rachel forget all about her "thorn in the flesh," Mrs. Gump.

That evening Wilma didn't pick up her children until just before supper, so Tom invited her and her children to eat with them.

"That sounds nice," Wilma said. "I love my work but eating someone else's food sounds downright restful. Packing all that merchandise around wears a body out."

Max arrived just before they ate, and as usual his children paid no attention to his arrival. "I just heard about a man who's taken sick," he told Tom. "Dr. Miller's treatin' him. Thought you might like to go take a look too."

If Tom were a dog, thought Rachel *his ears would have perked up.* "What's wrong with the man?" he asked.

"Don't rightly know. Seems he's perty bad off, though."

"Why don't you just leave it alone?" Rachel asked. "The other doctor is helping the man."

Tom gave her a long look. "If I can help the man, I'm ready," he said firmly.

Wilma Johnson chewed and swallowed her bite of baked potato. "I don't want to seem nosy, but why would you go see a sick man you don't know?"

"I bet you don't know Tom Dorland is a doctor," Max said. "A good one too. He healed my little Bonnie right up. He and Doc Miller don't agree how to make people well."

Wilma seemed overwhelmed with so much information. "Oh. Well, I don't know much about medicine. It's too complicated for me. Luckily we've always been well."

"Could you take me to the man's place after we finish eating?" Tom asked Max. "Or just tell me how to get there?"

"Shore. I'll show you the way. It's over past my place a few houses."

When Max gathered up his family, they took off down the street, Max carrying Eddie and Tom leading Willie and Bonnie.

"It must be handy being married to a doctor," Wilma said.

Rachel grinned. "It's nice being married to Tom but not because he's a doctor. He's just a nice man. As for him being a doctor, we haven't been sick so I don't see that side of him often."

"What about the other man, whose kids you care for? Why doesn't his wife keep them with her?"

Rachel sat down and told Wilma about Ruth Barer's death, and how Tom felt so terrible about it and felt she needn't have died.

"Remind me to call Tom when I get sick," Wilma said with a chuckle.

Soon Wilma called Alicia and Richard and hurried them down the board sidewalk. Now, with just her own, Rachel sat down to drink another cup of coffee. Three used to sound like so many children, but now they were hardly any at all.

Rachel fell asleep, but Tom awakened her about an hour later. "I got the man to promise not to let old Miller take any blood or give him any poison. How does that sound for starters?"

Rachel yawned and tried to think. "It might be a dangerous start," she said. "What if Dr. Miller comes after you?"

Tom grinned. "I'm ready anytime."

◆

Anytime came sooner than Rachel had hoped. They'd been playing with their own children for a change when someone pounded on the door.

"Just what do you think you're doing, telling my patients what I can and can't do?" he bellowed. "Are you aware that our country has just formed an organization that makes the guidelines for medical practice? It's called the American Medical Association. How would you like for me to turn you in to them? You might lose your license. Looks like that's what you're trying for anyway."

"I'm sorry you're offended," Tom told the older man. "But the kind of medicine you practice is extremely dangerous. Haven't you noticed a lot of your patients die?"

"Sure they die!" the man thundered. "If they'd get hold of me before they're so far gone, it would be different. Now you're trying to interfere. Doesn't take much delay to cost a man's life, you know."

"I'm not trying to cause you grief," Tom said. "Do you know that in Europe they've given up purging and bleeding? They've discovered it weakens rather than heals. When a person doesn't get better, American doctors bleed or purge again! The patient gets weaker, and so it goes until the patient dies. It hurts me a lot to see people die who don't need to. Mrs. Barer for one. Her children needed her so badly."

The doctor dropped heavily into a chair. "What are those so-called doctors in Europe doing for their patients that's so much better?"

Tom shook his head. "I'm not sure it's all that good either, but at least it doesn't kill them. They're using a mixture of brandy and milk internally and also as baths. They say that a fever is indication of too little vitality where you say it indicates too much. I'm not sure they're right either, but at least the European method isn't life-threatening."

The man got up. "I don't know why I'm sitting here listening to you—a young know-it-all telling me how to treat my patients. I suppose I've treated a hundred patients for every one of yours." He headed for the door and stopped before opening it. "I'll thank you not to interfere with my patients again—or I'll take further measures. Good day, Mr. Dorland."

Rachel felt chills run down her backbone. "That man wasn't bluffing, Tom," she said. "I think you'd better leave him alone and just take care of your own patients."

Tom looked shocked. "If you saw a tree falling on a man, wouldn't you tell him to move?"

Why would Tom choose to talk about trees at this moment? "Of course. Who wouldn't?"

Tom nodded. "That's what I'm doing, love. Telling them a tree is coming their way—and it'll kill them for sure."

All at once Rachel felt tired to the bone. "I have to go to bed, Tom. Tomorrow will be here long before I'm ready."

❧

Gabriel woke only once in the night, and Rachel felt good in the morning. "Just imagine what it's going to be like in the Resurrection," she told Tom as they cuddled before getting up. "No one will ever get tired. We'll be able to run all day, stay up forever, do anything and everything, and never get tired. And there won't be any weeds in our gardens."

"You forgot," Tom said. "There'll be no more pain nor sorrow nor crying nor death. I'm ready for it right now. But unfortunately we have to face life as it is today. You have half a million babies to take care of and I have half a million patients to make well." He hugged her close for a few seconds and then bounded out of bed.

Rachel barely had a big pot of oatmeal, dried apples, and cinnamon boiling when the Barer children arrived, then the Johnsons. Tommy awakened in time to eat with the herd, as Tom and Rachel had begun calling their large family.

After breakfast Rachel bathed her own three and the Barer four. The two Johnsons always seemed clean. She dressed the children, found them all something to play with, and sat down, wondering what to do for the short time before someone needed her.

She'd just decided to sew some simple thing for Mrs. Gump when someone banged on the door. She opened it to admit Dr. Miller. "Where is he?" the man roared. "Get your husband out here right now."

nine

Rachel felt weak. "He isn't here, sir. Could you tell me what's wrong?"

"My patient just dismissed me. That's what. Haven't you two ever heard of medical ethics? I guarantee he'll lose his license for this. I'll guarantee it, Mrs. Dorland." The man walked off down the street.

When Rachel came out of her shock, she discovered both Jesse and Gabriel crying. Before she got them picked up, Tommy and Eddie joined the chorus. Rachel grinned. *Crying is like measles,* she thought, *very contagious.*

She diapered all four babies, fed the twins, found toys for Tommy and Eddie, and put the twins on blankets on the floor. Then she started some bread. Kneading and pounding it relieved some of the tension Dr. Miller had brought. She smiled; with all the big batches of bread she had to make these days, she should be able to handle all the tensions in her life just by kneading. Of course it would help if she could work without being interrupted; today she had nine interruptions: two wanted drinks; four needed clean diapers; one wanted a toy; two more wanted to nurse, but they managed to wait until she got the bread set. Why did she think she could do any sewing with all these young ones?

When Tom appeared for dinner, Rachel told him about the good doctor's visit. "I know," he said gleefully. "I'm taking care of the sick man now. Isn't that great?"

"It didn't sound so wonderful to me. He talked as if you won't be taking care of anyone pretty soon."

"Don't you worry about it. If I can save a few lives, that's worth a little hassle, isn't it?"

He washed all the children and put them into their places at the table. Rachel dipped the vegetable soup into bowls and mugs. Everyone had a thick slice of bread liberally spread with butter, and they each had a glass of milk. No one said much while everyone ate his fill.

Tom kissed Rachel before he left for work. "Don't worry about a thing," he said. "My new patient is doing great. He'll be back at work in another day or two. If Doc had started purging and bleeding him, the man would have been a long time sick—or dead."

That evening another doctor, Dr. Couperous, visited them. "I didn't come here to judge or to chastise," he said, "but I'd like to hear your side of the story, Dr. Dorland."

Tom told him all his thoughts and feelings on the subject of medicine, including his feeling of the total inadequacy of medical knowledge in America. He told the man how the European medical community had learned long ago that purging and bleeding only weakened sick people and hastened death.

"Well—that's quite a load you're carrying," Dr. Couperous said when Tom finally finished. "But why do you choose to believe the European method of healing rather than our own?"

"Because I've watched people weaken and die from the so-called treatment we use. Tell me, Doctor, what do you see in your practice? Do the purges and bleeding bring a lot of good health to your patients?"

Dr. Couperous looked troubled for a moment, then smiled. "That's hard to answer, son. No two patients are alike."

"Well, do most of your patients get better? Do you keep bleeding them more and more? Or do you give them a chance to recover?"

"I—I uh—I guess I give them a chance to recover."

"Doesn't that tell you something? You have to let them recover from your healing? The Europeans used to treat as we do, but they've seen the error and are correcting it. Why do people have to die while we continue to hold on to the old antiquated ways?"

Dr. Couperous got up and held his right hand out to Tom. "I certainly credit you with sincerity in your beliefs," he said, "but that doesn't mean you're right. I plan to do a little studying into this myself. If I get it figured out I'll get back to you." He lowered his voice as if saying something confidential. "In the meantime, why don't you just care for your own patients? Remember, those people chose their doctor, as your patients chose you. I think that's the only way we can have peace in our little town, Dorland."

Tom pushed his hair off his forehead and grinned wearily. "I'll try, Dr. Couperous. I'll do my best."

Rachel shook her head when the doctor left. "He's right, Tom. You better treat your patients and let the other doctors treat theirs. You can't cure the entire medical profession all by yourself. If you don't stop preaching and just be a doctor, you'll be in big trouble."

Tom didn't look worried. "I think Dr. Couperous will find I'm right."

Rachel felt worried. A lot worried. "Just do what he asked, all right, Tom? Otherwise you'll be looking for a new kind of job."

Rachel lost count of the times Gabriel got her up that night, and the next morning she wanted to pull the covers over her head and sleep all day. But she struggled out of bed and made breakfast for nine children, Max Barer, Tom, and herself. A loaf and a half of bread disappeared for breakfast as well as the oatmeal, milk, and coffee.

She'd bathed Gabriel, Jesse, and Tommy, when Deborah Cline, the Sunday School superintendent, came up the sidewalk and knocked on the door. Rachel put the babies down where they could play and watch the others play, and then she put on the coffee pot.

"It's nice to talk to an adult once in a while," Rachel said, handing a steaming mug to Deborah. "How's Sunday School going these days?"

Deborah took a sip from her mug. "Not very well. In fact, that's why I'm here. I need a teacher for the three- and four-year-olds. I thought since you're with them all the time you'd be perfect." She gave a quiet laugh. "You probably think like them by now."

Rachel's heart sank into her shoes. She looked forward to her lessons with adults. Frankly, she saw enough of tiny children during the week. Her brain needed a rest and also a challenge. She smiled at her guest. "Do you realize I take care of nine children every day all day? And that four of them are one year old and under? And that I feed all those children three times a day? As well as wash clothes for most of them?" She shook her head at the thought. "Tom comes home late in the afternoon and watches the children while I wash clothes. By the time I get the children into bed and my work finished, I barely have strength to crawl into my own bed."

Deborah smiled brightly. "No doubt you're a busy person. But I've heard if you want something done, ask a busy person."

Rachel shook her head. "I can't do it, Deborah. I just can't."

"What if I can't find anyone else?"

"You can. Ask one of the children's mothers. How about Wilma Johnson? Alicia must be in that group."

"I'll do my best," Deborah said as she went out, "but most people don't care that much, even about their own children."

≈

That evening Tom congratulated Rachel for actually having

the backbone to say no. "You may as well stop before you kill yourself," he said, "because they'll never stop hounding you until you do."

But the next morning Deborah returned, shaking her head sadly. "Not a one of them will do it. Wilma Johnson said she works hard during the day and can't stay up late preparing."

"She doesn't work as hard as I," Rachel said. "And many times I make her supper as well as her children's. I work from the moment I get up in the morning until I fall into bed totally exhausted at night."

"Look," Deborah said, "you could spend fifteen minutes a day while the children nap and never miss the time."

Rachel felt herself getting sucked in. "Why don't you do it?" she asked. "You can't possibly be as busy as I."

Deborah looked at Rachel as if she were a little child. "You know I have to be in the adult department, Rachel. You see me there every week."

Finally, Rachel agreed to give it a try.

Tom frowned when Rachel told him at dinner. "You didn't have to do it, love. We don't even have a child in there and if the parents don't care, why should you? Let them take their youngsters with them and watch them themselves."

"Well, I'm only giving it a try."

After Tom left she put the children down for naps and pulled out the lesson book. Gabriel interrupted before she finished the first page. Then Jesse. When she finished with the twins, she tried again to study the book, but she fell asleep on the second page. It seemed she'd just sat down when the children awakened, eager and ready for something to do.

☙

That night Tom almost floated in his excitement over his new patient. "He's well, Rachel. He's going back to work tomorrow. Aren't you glad old Miller didn't sink his hooks into the man?"

"How are your other patients?"

A broad grin split his face. "No one's in danger. All are better than they were when I started seeing them. Not bad, huh?"

"Not bad. If you just don't get into big trouble with the other doctors."

"I won't. And listen to this. I have a half-dozen new patients who specifically came to me because I don't purge and bleed."

Rachel wasn't sure that was all good news either. What would the other doctors say? She didn't say anymore but hurried to get started on the washing.

When she put Gabriel to bed that night, hopefully for the last time, she decided to spend a little time on the Sunday School lesson, but she fell asleep within five minutes. She slept in the chair until Gabriel wakened a few hours later.

☙

Saturday Rachel realized she had to teach those children tomorrow at church. She put the children down after dinner and forced herself to concentrate on the lesson. She didn't fall asleep, but her mind wasn't razor sharp either. When the children awakened, she realized she'd had all the preparation she'd get.

That night Wilma Johnson joined the large family for supper again. As they ate, Rachel noticed Max Barer looked cleaner and neater than she'd ever seen him. When had all this happened? Evidently it was good for him to see how clean she kept the children. Watching him, she deduced his manners had also improved considerably. She felt a rosy glow, the glow of helping someone to a better life, even if only a little better.

The next morning Rachel felt so tired she forgot all about

her teaching assignment. When they arrived at the church, Deborah Cline hurried over to them. "I thought you'd never come," Deborah said. "You're supposed to be here fifteen minutes early, you know."

Rachel felt as though she'd been hit, right in the pit of her stomach. And she hadn't even brought the book! "Oh no," she wailed. "I forgot the lesson book."

"Oh well," Deborah purred. "You don't use the book to teach anyway. Come on, I'll take you to your room."

Soon Rachel faced fifteen tiny scrubbed faces, all looking at her expectantly.

"Tell them good morning," Deborah whispered. "I'll get out of your way so you can get busy." She disappeared through the doorway.

Rachel had never even watched anyone work in this department. She got on her knees and told the children the lesson was about a little boy with five stones. As soon as she said it she realized she didn't want to teach those tiny children about a killing. She'd teach them about Jesus feeding the five thousand.

"I have to potty," a little boy said. No sooner had he said it than a dark stain appeared on his overalls. Now what was she supposed to do? She decided she'd ignore the problem and teach the class.

"Did you know Jesus fed a whole lot of people all the bread and fish they could eat one day when they were hungry?" she asked the children.

"I'm hungry," a small girl said. "I want bread and fish." Soon three more children announced they were hungry too.

"I don't have anything here to eat," Rachel said, "but let's learn how Jesus fed so many people."

"I want fish," a little boy said. Then he opened up his mouth and bellowed. "Bawww."

A moment later every child in the group was crying. Rachel

felt like walking out and letting them cry, but she knew that wasn't the best solution to her problem. As the children screamed, she discovered she had a splitting headache, the kind a person gets from lack of sleep.

"Rachel's my best friend," a little voice chirped into the bedlam. Rachel looked up and noticed Alicia for the first time.

"Yes, Alicia comes to my house to play every day. Alicia, tell me what you like best about coming to my house."

Alicia stood up importantly. "I like Rachel's potato soup and fat bread."

"I want fat bread," someone yelled after a brief silence. Then everyone wanted fat bread.

"Do you usually eat in Sunday School?" Rachel asked, afraid to hear the answer.

"Yes," a little girl sitting beside Alicia yelled. "We eat fat bread." She looked at Alicia. "What's fat bread?"

"It's big fat slices of bread so soft your finger goes right through it. It has lots of butter on it. It runs all over your hands."

Ten mouths opened and yelled for fat bread. Rachel knew for certain Deborah would soon be here asking what was happening. If only Rachel could get the children interested in something besides eating. What could she talk about?

"Do you know who Jesus is?" she asked hopefully.

"He's the baby that slept in the hay."

"He's the baby who couldn't cry."

Timmy, one of the larger boys, pointed to the child who'd wet his pants, Duane. "There he is. There's a baby who didn't cry. He's Jesus! Jesus wets his pants." He laughed so hard he fell off his chair.

Duane's eyes grew red, his lip quivered, and he burst into tears. "No," he sobbed.

"Yes, you are," Timmy said. "And you can't cry either."

Duane opened his mouth and his lips quivered, but he didn't make another sound.

Rachel squatted beside him. "I wouldn't mind being called Jesus," she said softly. "Did you know Jesus made our world? And He made us? And He loves us even more than our mamas and papas do?"

Timmy pointed at her. "Jesus, Jesus, Jesus," he shouted, laughing some more. Most of the children took up the chant- -and pointed at her as Timmy did. "Jesus, Jesus, teacher's Jesus."

Oh, when was this terrible hour going to be over? Rachel decided the best thing to do would be to ignore the name-calling and get on with something about Jesus. "Do you know where Jesus lives?" she finally managed to ask.

"Jesus lives at your house because you're Jesus!" Timmy shouted merrily.

"Jesus lives in heaven way up in the sky," Rachel told them. "But He lives somewhere else too. Do you know where that is?"

"At your house with a hunnerd younguns."

"Jesus does live at my house," Rachel said softly so they'd have to be quiet to hear. "He lives at your house too," she went on, "because He lives in your heart. He lives in each of our hearts where He can love us all the time."

"You don't live at my house, Jesus," Timmy yelled.

Just then the door opened, and Tom came in with three babies in his arms. "Gabriel needs you," he said quietly.

"I can't do it now," she said desperately. "Unless you can take over here."

"Don't bother Jesus," Timmy said. "Jesus is helping us."

Tom looked into Rachel's eyes. "Jesus?"

She rolled her eyes. "Don't ask. Could you sing with them or something until I finish?"

"Sure. Why don't you go over behind those cupboards. I

see a chair over there."

She took Gabriel, leaving Tommy and Jesse in Tom's arms, and settled into a chair in semi-privacy.

"We want Jesus!" Timmy yelled at the top of his lungs. The other children all joined the chorus.

"Hush!" Tom bellowed after a full minute of uproar. "It's not nice to call Mrs. Dorland Jesus. Jesus is our God. Didn't you know that?"

"She told us to call her Jesus," Timmy said in a subdued voice.

"Let's sing about Jesus," Tom said, then led them in some children's songs.

Some of the children sang with Tom, but Timmy refused even to try. "She told us to call her Jesus," he whimpered over and over.

Finally the closing bell rang, and the parents collected their children. "Did you have fun in Sunday School today?" Rachel heard Timmy's mother ask.

Rachel listened for Timmy's response. "Yes. But that bad man wouldn't let us talk to Jesus." Hearing the boy's answer she shuddered. *Tell me I didn't hopelessly confuse this little boy, God. And forgive me for whatever I said to make him think I was Jesus. Straighten his thinking out. Help him to understand about who You are. Please.*

Rachel didn't hear a word of the sermon that day. She kept hearing Timmy telling his mother that Tom wouldn't let him talk to Jesus.

When they finally began their short walk home, Tom with Tommy and Gabriel in his arms and she with Jesse, Tom looked up at the white sky. "It's really cold," he said. "Rain's the usual here, but it feels as if it could snow any minute. We'd better hurry home before someone freezes."

Then he raised quizzical eyebrows at her. "What's this about you being Jesus?"

Rachel didn't feel like going into it. "Could we talk about it later?" she asked. "It was awful, Tom. Not only was I not prepared, but those tiny little children ran the class. They wouldn't let me tell them anything." Then she remembered the fat bread and told him about that. "Everyone of them was crying, really crying, for fat bread. I'll admit Alicia made it sound pretty good. For a long time I couldn't get the kids to think about anything but food. Then I asked them who Jesus is. Timmy pointed at Duane and called him Jesus. Everyone laughed until Duane cried. I cuddled him and told him I'd like to be called Jesus, that Jesus made our world and us and loves us better than anyone, even our mamas and papas." She shrugged. "So Timmy started everyone calling me Jesus and I couldn't stop them."

ten

Tom thought the story funny. "Children have been besting their elders forever, love. Don't give it another thought."

Rachel always felt strange on Sunday, cooking a meal for just the three of them. It seemed there weren't enough people to bother with. Yet it felt good to relax and not have to keep so many plates filled and children happy.

After they ate, they put the three babies down for naps, and Rachel collapsed on her bed too. She couldn't hold her head up one more minute or keep her eyes open. Working so hard had totally drained her, but that had been a picnic compared to what she'd been through at church.

Something awakened her later; after sleeping so hard, she felt disoriented. Listening a moment, she heard low voices buzzing in the front room. She decided she'd better get up and see who'd come calling.

Rachel straightened her hair a little and went downstairs. Several couples sat in a small group visiting, but when she entered, the talking stopped. "Hello," she said cheerily, though she had a strange feeling. "What a nice surprise to see all of you here."

Tom stood and winked at her. "Yes, recently I've been having all the company, but today these people came just to see you." He placed her in the chair he'd vacated, sat on the floor beside it, and reached for her hand.

"What can I do for you people?" Rachel asked. "What on earth could bring you all out on such a cold afternoon?"

The people all looked at each other. Some cleared their throats, some coughed, some said nothing. "We understand

you want to be called Jesus," a tall, thin man finally barked
out.

Oh no! That had to get all over the church, didn't it? She
tried to smile and answer light-heartedly. "I'm afraid your
children have gotten that all mixed up. I didn't say that nor
do I want to be called Jesus—now or ever." She looked at
their sober faces and couldn't help laughing. She choked it
off as soon as possible. "A thought just crossed my mind,"
she said clearly. "The Bible says there will be lots of men
claiming to be Christ, but I haven't read about women saying such foolish things."

A long silence followed her words. Then the people began looking at each other again as if asking what they should
do now.

"Well, now," a short plump man finally said, "why don't
you tell us exactly what happened."

Rachel didn't feel like going through it again. It had been
humiliating enough telling Tom. She looked beseechingly
into his eyes, wanting to ask if she really had to explain the
innocent remark.

"Why don't I just explain it?" Tom asked, propelling himself to a commanding position, standing over the people.
"For starters, your children weren't very well-behaved at
church today. One of them called the smallest child in the
room Jesus. The other children took it up and the little boy
cried. My wife had him almost quieted when the first child
started again. Again the other children joined in, picking on
the tiny boy. My wife cuddled the child in her arms and told
him she wouldn't mind being called Jesus, as He created
the world and made each of us and loves us even more than
our mamas and papas do. The children misunderstood and
thought she was asking them to call her Jesus." He looked
from face to face. "That's about it. Does she sound like a
bad woman to you? Maybe one who shouldn't be allowed

in a room alone with your children?"

Another long silence followed Tom's remarks. Finally a woman met his eyes. "We didn't say anything like that, Dr. Dorland. We just wanted to hear how it happened. Now we understand, I think we all agree she's an excellent person to leave our children with."

Rachel didn't know whether to be glad or sad. She really didn't want to get fired from the teaching position, but she hoped never to be stuck in a room alone with all those children again.

The next morning all of Rachel's charges arrived right on time, and she spent her time and energy keeping everyone comfortable and happy. That included keeping Tommy and Eddie from sticking their fingers into the twins' eyes, and stopping Alicia from pushing Tommy and Eddie over, and carefully watching all the children to keep the blocks from flying.

At noon Tom happily announced three new patients. "I'm nearing a full load," he said. "I guess between us we have far more than a full load already."

Rachel laughed. "And to think, I never get paid for my work."

No one left that night until darkness fell, so Max offered to walk Wilma Johnson home. They headed off down the sidewalk, two adults with six children running around them.

≈

Every day Tom had more new patients until he couldn't get through early enough to help Rachel. She did the washing and watched the children too, but it took more than twice as long. She started as soon as everyone went down for naps and finished about when Tom got home, around six-thirty. They fixed supper together, a procedure that soon became routine.

Rachel hadn't thought she could possibly be any more

tired, but she learned it was possible. She dragged herself through the evening, thinking only of getting the children and then herself into bed.

When her head hit the pillow her eyes snapped shut, not to wake again until someone needed to be fed. The next morning she overslept and had to hurry to have things ready for everyone.

That day at dinner Tom talked with excitement. "People are seeing what's happening to the purged patients. They don't like what they see so they're coming to me. Already I have far more than my share of the patients in this town. I'm about ready to teach those big boys a lesson."

But Dr. Miller arrived that evening before Tom got home. "What is your husband telling the people, to be able to steal them from me?" he asked.

Rachel shook her head. "I have no idea, Dr. Miller. You'll have to come after supper if you want to talk to Tom. He's very busy these days."

The man looked at her suspiciously. "Who's helping you with the children?"

"I do it alone—what gets done," she said. "Tom's been getting so many new patients he can't help much any more."

Dr. Miller nodded. "That's why I'm here, young woman. And I'm staying until I talk to him."

The doctor ended up talking to Tom while they fixed supper. "You'd better just come clean and tell me what you've been saying to the people around town," he insisted. "My patient load has dwindled while yours has soared. Don't try to tell me this is coincidence. What have you been telling them?"

Tom didn't seem the least bothered by the man's pique. "I'm not saying anything. Why don't you go ask your old patients why they came to me? I'll tell you the truth, Doctor, I'd never accept another doctor's patients unless the people had good reason for switching. And they do."

"Like what?"

"Like they're tired of paying someone to make them sicker—and they see people dying who should live. You're going to have to learn new methods of treating, Doctor. Why don't you do it before you lose any more patients?"

"Because my methods are right. There are seven or eight doctors in Oregon City, Dorland, and you're one against the rest. Doesn't that tell you anything?"

Tom grinned. "Yeah. It tells me I'm not getting through to them as quickly as I wish."

The man lumbered to his feet. "Well, listen to what I'm telling you. If you don't keep your quackish ideas to yourself we're going to have you run out of town—and that's a promise." He closed the door with a little more force than necessary.

"Tom," Rachel said, "doesn't that bother you at all?"

"Yes, it does," Tom said quietly. "It bothers me more than I can say to see those outdated windbags killing people off right and left and calling it medicine."

Rachel felt altogether too tired to argue, so they fed the children, finally sent them home, and put their own babies to bed. Rachel barely kept her eyes open until she pulled the covers up.

ها

The next morning she thought she simply couldn't climb out of bed. But she had to. The herd of children would be here in half an hour whether she was ready or not.

She fed all the children, bathed the usual ones, and dressed them in clean clothes. Then she kept falling asleep as she sat with them helping them play and making sure no one got hurt.

A little later Papa dropped by. "I just had to see what new and exciting things you're doing now," he said. "How many new babies do you have?"

"Altogether I have nine, Papa. And I'm so tired I've been falling asleep watching them."

"You aren't still letting that old crow bully you around, are you?" he asked just as someone knocked on the door.

Rachel let Mrs. Gump in. "Looks like you have everything under control here," she said with a smile.

"It's better," Rachel said. "I can't figure why I'm so terribly tired all the time, though."

"You're getting bored with not enough to keep you busy, that's why. I'd like to see you sewing for the Society again. Doing the lovely work you do, I'm sure you miss it."

Rachel shook her head. "I can't do it right now. You can't imagine how it is here. If I went up into the bedroom to sew, these children would not only blind the babies, but tear each other into small pieces." She smiled and shook her head again. "The children have to come first." Then she brightened. "I just thought how I could sew," she said. "I'd be more than glad to sew as long as you'd stay and watch the children."

Mrs. Gump looked surprised but didn't respond to the suggestion. "Well," she said in a surprisingly kind voice, "you just watch for a spare minute or two and use them to sew some clothes." She patted Rachel on the arm. "You're an angel, you know, and we all appreciate you."

After the woman left, Papa had plenty of suggestions for ways for Rachel to handle the pushy woman. Rachel didn't accept any of them.

2a

Rachel grew more exhausted each day until one day she glanced at the calendar and noticed Christmas would arrive in three days. She didn't have the strength to even consider a gift for Tom or her three babies. Maybe no one else would remember. Tom didn't mention the holiday until everyone had gone home on Christmas Eve. Rachel hurried the babies to bed so she could drop into her own bed, hoping to get a little extra rest.

But he caught her before she got in bed and held her close. "Do you remember what day this is?" he asked.

She couldn't tell an untruth so she nodded. "I hoped no one else would remember," she said. "I've been far too exhausted to celebrate anything, even our precious Lord's birth." She looked toward the ceiling. "Forgive me, dear God. I'm just so tired trying to do all You ask me to that I think I can't get through another day."

Tom ran into the extra bedroom and returned with a package. "Unwrap it," he instructed, pushing her onto the edge of the bed.

She did and found a beautiful cream-colored wool coat. "Oh, Tom, it's beautiful. I'm so sorry I didn't get you anything."

He grinned. "How could you? I wouldn't have bought you anything if I'd had to take nine children with me." He held her close and stroked her hair away from her face. "The storekeeper thought I was pretty tight when I wouldn't even consider a fur coat. But I knew how you'd feel about that."

Tom was truly the most thoughtful man in the world. "Thank you again, Tom. You knew I'd never wear a fur coat, didn't you?" She shuddered. "I don't understand how anyone could ever take a little animal's coat and wear it as if it were hers." She shuddered again. "It's even worse when you realize it takes many little animals' coats to make just one for a person." After a few minutes of cuddling, they climbed into bed and Rachel fell asleep almost instantly.

The next morning the Barer children came as usual, but Wilma Johnson didn't have to work. No one mentioned Christmas, so Rachel guessed Max Barer was skipping it too.

Tom had some patients he had to see, so the day was nearly like all others. Rachel fixed soup and sandwiches for dinner. She should have started bread in the morning, but she hadn't had time, so she did the heavy job while the soup cooked. She made six loaves every other day now that her family had grown so large. When she'd kneaded the large mass of dough fifteen minutes, she put it back into the large dish pan, set it on top of the warming oven, and laid a clean dish towel over it. She'd be lucky if it was ready for supper. Oh well, she could always make biscuits.

Tom came home exuberant, and Rachel felt almost irritated at him. Here she was, stuck with all these children, and he got to go out and do the job he'd trained for and loved.

"I picked up two new patients this morning," he said, shaking his head. "I can't take any more unless I work longer, maybe going back in the evenings."

"Please don't! I need you so badly. I have to do the washing alone now and watch the young ones. It's hard, Tom."

He pulled her to him and held her for a long minute. "Why don't you quit and just care for our babies?" he asked. "No one can make you do something that's too hard for you."

Tom's suggestion felt better than almost anything Rachel had ever heard. Her head pounded and her eyes hurt, she felt so tired. She felt overwhelmed and exhausted all the time. But who would watch the children? She hadn't done it because she'd thought it would be fun. She'd done it because these people were desperate. She shook her head. "I'm stuck with the children. They need me badly. But do you think I could get out of teaching that class? I don't have a minute to prepare the lesson, and I don't want to do it anyway."

"Consider it done. I'll stop by and tell Deborah Cline this afternoon. She won't be able to bully me into backing down."

Rachel began the washing as soon as she put the children down for naps. If they'd all sleep an hour it would help but they never did. She felt such a tremendous relief from Tom's promise to get her out of teaching the Sunday School class that she didn't feel quite so tired as she had before.

She'd washed most of the diapers when someone knocked on the door. *Why couldn't they have waited until the children awakened?* It was so hard to watch the youngsters and wash clothes too. She definitely couldn't hang the clothes, even in the spare bedroom, while the children were here. That job had to wait until Tom got home or the children went home. Then they never got dry before the children returned in the morning.

The person waiting knocked again, and when Rachel opened the door she wished she hadn't. The Sunday School superintendent, Deborah Cline, stood there wearing a wide smile. "Good afternoon," she said, shaking snow from her coat and stepping inside. "Did you know it's snowing outside? It's going to be a hard winter. I'm here to tell on your bad husband. Do you know what he did? He tried to tell me you don't want to teach that class of little ones anymore." She smiled again and winked at Rachel. "When a person does such a grand job you know they have to love it, isn't that right?"

Rachel swallowed the rock that formed in her throat. "I asked Tom to stop and tell you," she said, feeling guiltier every second. "I don't have time to do it, and I haven't been around three- and four-year-olds much at all. I don't know how to handle them."

"Don't worry about a thing," Deborah said. "Even if you do it without preparation you'll do better than anyone else."

"Tom can't take care of our own three babies alone, Deborah, and I enjoy my own class after being with children all week. I just can't do it. I'm sorry."

Deborah looked as if she might cry. "I guess the poor little tykes won't have a Sunday School then. Not one person in our entire church cares enough to sacrifice one hour for them."

Inasmuch as you've done it for the least of these you've done it for Me. Rachel felt like screaming at Deborah. She felt like yelling at God a little too. Why did He expect her to do everything?

Then her thoughts quieted. Who would do it if she didn't? Was it right to deny the little ones their chance to learn about God? But a lot of women didn't have children of their own to care for—and no one had three as young as hers.

"Well," Deborah's voice penetrated Rachel's thoughts, "I'm glad to see you've reconsidered. Just teach them whatever you want, Rachel. Make it as easy on yourself as possible. Goodbye—and thanks. You're an angel." Deborah Cline marched across the porch, down the steps, and over the wooden sidewalk, which was nearly covered with snow; she had reached the street before Rachel collected herself enough to say a word.

Rachel bent over the washboard, picked up a little shirt, and gave it three scrubs on the board before Gabriel's stentorian voice called, awakening all the other children too.

The rest of the afternoon consisted of caring for children, scrubbing one or two garments, caring for children, scrubbing another garment, and on and on. And on top of all this she had to teach that class of little rebels.

About five o'clock Rachel noticed another girl coming up the steps. She opened the door to a young mother she'd met at the store, Melissa Witlow. "I need to talk to someone," the plump, dark-haired woman said. "Is your husband here? Or should I talk to you?"

Rachel swallowed and continued rocking twelve-month-old Eddie Barer on her hip. "I'm not sure," she said. "What do you need to talk about? And no, Tom isn't here."

When tears glistened on the woman's eyelashes, Rachel's

heart melted within her. She steered Melissa to the settle, went after a mug of coffee for her trembling guest, then sat in the rocker facing her. "How can I help you?" she asked after giving the woman time to collect herself.

Melissa hiccupped twice, then sat quietly for another moment, gathering strength. Then she leaned forward. "Homer is too hard on our children. He hurts me too. Oh, Rachel, what can I do?" She pulled her long sleeve above her elbow, exposing a dark bruise.

"Did he do that?" Rachel asked, horrified.

"Yes, he does it continually. The children are bruised and their backs have long red welts most of the time. What can I do, Rachel? I have to protect my children."

eleven

Rachel had never seen or heard of anything like this. "I don't know, Melissa," she whispered. "Maybe you should talk to the minister."

"I already did," Melissa said. "He said for me and the children to try harder to please Homer." She raised teary eyes to meet Rachel's blue ones. "We've tried so hard, Rachel. We really have. What happens is that he goes to the saloon and drinks awhile. When he comes home he's mad at everyone. That's when he hurts us. He calls me horrible names too." She lost control and cried hard for a few minutes. When she finally raised her head, Rachel saw determination in her eyes.

"I'm going to leave him," Melissa said. "Before I kill him, or he kills one of us. It's worse than I can tell you, Rachel. Will you help me?"

"How could I help?"

"You can let us come here. Or you can take the children." Tears threatened again. "I've been thinking about this for two years," Melissa said. "We don't have any place to go but we have to get out."

"But remember your wedding vows? What God has joined together, let no man put asunder. Christians don't get divorced, Melissa."

Melissa tossed her head. "I won't be a Christian then. I'm not anyway. Rachel, I have to get out and get my babies out too."

"Melissa, let's pray about this."

Melissa shook her head. "I've been praying about it for

three years but God doesn't answer. If He doesn't want to help, I have to help myself."

Tears filled Rachel's eyes and ran over. She put Eddie on the floor and hugged Melissa tightly. "I'm so sorry," she whispered into Melissa's ear. "But this is new to me. You've been thinking about it a long time, but I've never known anyone who got a divorce. Marriage is sacred, you know. But you can't let him hurt your children. Let me talk to Tom about this and let you know soon."

Melissa nodded. "I guess. Hurry, though, Rachel." She lowered her head and ran through the door into the cold snowy world.

Rachel could hardly concentrate on forming the bread dough into the six loaves, and when she diapered the babies, she changed Gabriel, Jesse, Eddie, and then Gabriel again, forgetting Tommy. She even forgot all about Deborah Cline and the little ones' Sunday School class.

When Tom finally came home, she forgot the washing that had to be hung somewhere. But she didn't forget to tell Tom about the Witlow family. "What can we do?" she asked when she finished. "What's the right thing?"

"First off, we don't have a place for three more people in our house," Tom said. "Second, I'd have to think a long time before advising anyone to break up a marriage. Let's pray about it."

They knelt down with children running and yelling all around them, put their arms around each other with their cheeks touching so they could hear each other, and talked to their dearest Friend. They told Him they had no idea what was right, except that they knew He didn't want Homer harming any of his family. They asked Him to show them what they should do. Then they stayed quietly on their knees waiting for His answer.

But all they heard were nine children yelling, laughing, and crying. Crying! Gabriel. Rachel jumped up and gathered him into her arms. "Tom," she whispered as she sat in the rocker nursing the hungry baby, "have I ever told you how much I appreciate your love and kindness to me? And our babies?" Then she laughed. "And to all the others I keep bringing into the house?"

"I appreciate you, too," he said softly. "When I first knew you I thought you were the most spoiled girl I'd ever met—but look at you now! You have the biggest heart in the West; if it were visible it would be a medical phenomenon." He leaned over her shoulder and kissed her cheek. "But we still have a problem," he said. "And we don't know how to solve it so we'll just wait on the Lord."

Tom watched the youngsters and fixed some split pea soup to go with the fresh bread, while Rachel hung the clothes in the extra bedroom. When she finished, she stood looking out the window, wishing she could go outside and build a snowman, be a child with no responsibilities. But that wouldn't solve any problems.

"Thank You, Lord, for being so good to us," she prayed out loud. "Thank You for giving me such a wonderful man, one who loves You as I do, and loves me with all his heart. Thank You too for giving us our precious little boys and all the other little children You've given us to love. Help me to always do Your will, exactly as You want me to. And help the Witlows solve their problems, Father. Help them to love You first, then each other with all their hearts. Thank You, in Jesus' precious name. I love You, Father."

After supper everyone went home, and Rachel couldn't wait until she had her family all in bed and could go to sleep herself. She felt as if she couldn't drag herself even as far as the bed.

Tom and Rachel prayed for Melissa and Homer Witlow again before they climbed into the soft feather bed. "Now we don't make a move until we hear from God," Tom said. "Agreed?"

"Yes," Rachel said, more asleep than awake.

ֆ

The next morning four doctors Rachel had never seen arrived before Tom left to go on his rounds. He opened the door and welcomed them. Then he called Rachel and introduced the doctors to her.

"I didn't realize you had such a lovely wife at home," the oldest and tallest one said. "Or that you had such a large family. I guess you need lots of patients to support a brood like this."

Tom laughed, sounding comfortable. "They aren't all ours, Doctor. Most of them are missionary projects my wife has taken on." He cast a loving glance Rachel's way. "People seem to gravitate to her when they have a problem. Keeps her plenty busy."

"Well, we're sorry to intrude on such a fine thing, but we need to talk to you both."

"Come into the kitchen," Tom said, "and we can sit around the table." Five minutes later they all had coffee and Rachel sat down beside Tom.

"Well, I want to wish every one of you a happy new year," a middle-aged man with blond hair and mustache said. "But that's not why we're here."

Rachel started. With her responsibilities she didn't pay much attention to the calendar. *January 1, 1862!* She could hardly believe it.

"The doctors of the community met last night," the same man continued, "and decided your brand of medicine isn't acceptable. They voted to ask you to either practice the accepted medical procedures, leave the area, or find some other way to earn a living."

Rachel felt as if the man had punched a big fist into her

diaphragm but Tom didn't look the least upset.

"Why is this, gentlemen?" he asked in a kind voice.

"Because we fear for the people of Oregon City. They deserve the best medical care available."

Tom laughed. "I couldn't agree with you more. But that seems to be the extent of our agreement. I have a suggestion, though. I'd be glad to share all my records with you gentlemen, if you'd do the same for me. It would be simple to figure out which method has the highest percentage of cures—and also where the deaths are coming from."

The men began shaking their heads one by one. "Medical ethics prevent doctors from sharing information on their patients, Dorland. I thought you'd know that. Patient confidentiality, you know."

"Come on. You fellows know that's no problem. You've all had physicians' consultations. Isn't that what this will be? Or we could get permission from our patients. Most of them would gladly release their records. I may as well be frank with you. If we do this and find my methods are causing my patients harm, I'll gladly switch. My only desire is to do the very best for my patients that's possible. But— that's the only condition under which I'll change my method of practice."

The doctors all looked uncomfortable except Tom, who seemed to be enjoying the meeting. One of them stood to his feet and the others followed suit. "We'll have to take this back to the committee," the older one said. "It's highly irregular, you know."

Tom stood too and shook each man's hand. "I realize this doesn't happen every day," he agreed. "But doctors don't get asked to change their profession every day either. You decide what you'd like to do and get back to me. Don't you think you owe me at least that? And thank you for coming."

After they left, Tom kissed Rachel on the cheek. "I haven't

forgotten your friend Melissa. Keep praying."

❧

Rachel prayed for Melissa and her family every time she thought about them—while she bathed children, while she swept the house, while she smoothed out fights, while she prepared dinner. She also thought of the four grim callers of the morning. She tried not to think about them, but she couldn't help it.

That afternoon when Wilma Johnson came after her children, she edged Rachel into the kitchen. "Guess what I just learned?" she whispered. Not waiting for an answer she went on. "I just learned that my husband didn't make it to Missouri. Someone killed him and took his horse and everything." She looked at Rachel, almost glared at her. "And I don't even care." She called her children and marched down the snowy sidewalk with them. Rachel sat down to absorb the news.

❧

A few days later when Tom came home for dinner, he looked exuberant. "I broke a high fever today with cool milk-and-water baths. The child is going to be all right." He grabbed Rachel and pulled her to him for a quick hug. "I'm on the right track, love!"

The thought crossed Rachel's mind that he might be through finding the right track soon, but she didn't dampen his enthusiasm.

Together they washed up all the children, put them in their places, and fed them. They knew how to do it quickly by this time.

After Tom left, Rachel put the children down for their naps and began the washing. Such hard work, so tiring, so routine, so boring. But it was easier now than when the children awoke. She began scrubbing diapers. She had about sixty to wash every day for the four babies. And it would be a long time before any of them were out of diapers. When she finished the diapers, she had lots of other clothes to wash for her own family and also the Barers.

Tom got home a little early that night and cheerfully began supper while Rachel hung the clothes in the upstairs bedroom. She knew it must be getting terribly cold outside when the room was so cold she needed a heavy coat to hang the clothes, her fingers were so cold they'd hardly grasp a clothespin, and the clothes didn't dry well either.

About the time they finished feeding the children, Max Barer came. Rachel gave him a plate of food. Then Wilma Johnson came and gathered up her two, refusing the food Rachel offered.

"Wait a minute," Max said through a mouthful of venison stew, "and I'll walk you home and build a fire for you."

Wilma smiled as if pleased and waited.

Tom glanced at Rachel and winked.

When everyone had cleared out, Tom pulled Rachel into his lap. "Did you notice anything tonight?" he asked.

"You mean Max and Wilma?"

He bit her ear. "Yes, I mean Max and Wilma. Think something's going on?"

"Could be. I'm not sure, though. She seems a little more—uh—educated than he is or something. Besides, she just learned her husband died."

"Don't doubt it, love. If the two of them get together, that could solve most of your problems."

As they discussed what life would be like with just their own family, a loud knocking on the door brought them back to the present.

Tom opened the door and Melissa Witlow burst through, covered with snow and followed by her two children, about three and six. Melissa had a pillowcase filled with something.

"We're here," she announced. "I hope you won't throw us out." With that she threw herself into the rocker, buried her face in her hands, and burst into loud sobs. Her two children stood watching their mother, their faces screwed into mirror images of her sad countenance.

Tom looked at Rachel and raised his eyebrows, as if to ask what was going on. Rachel shook her head. He'd said they had no place for three more people and he'd been right.

Rachel moved to Melissa's side and knelt beside the rocker. "Can you tell us what happened?" she asked quietly.

Melissa didn't look up, only shook her head.

The little girl finally opened her mouth and let out one loud bellow after another. Tom scooped her into his arms and sat on the settle. He pulled her head to his chest and patted it gently. The little girl cried louder than ever.

Finally, Melissa struggled to her feet and took the girl. "We're all right now, honey. Don't be afraid." The little girl huddled close to her mother, hiccupping every few seconds.

Rachel pulled the little boy to her. "Are you all right?" she asked quietly. He nodded. "It looks as if you haven't been having a very good time lately," she added. He shook his head.

Tom pulled a big slice of bread from the bread box, buttered it, and spread strawberry jam on it, then looked at the children. "Anyone hungry for some of my wife's good bread and jam?"

The little girl wiggled down from Melissa's arms, and the boy moved toward Tom. Tom put the children onto chairs, cut the bread in half, and put it on small plates before the children. The little girl grabbed the bread and shoved half of it into her small mouth. The boy watched her and did the same.

Tom looked surprised. "Those little ones are hungry!" he said.

Rachel turned back to Melissa. "Are you hungry too?"

Melissa shook her head no. "But we haven't had anything to eat since breakfast," she whispered.

"I'd better fix something then," Rachel said. As she moved toward the kitchen she realized how tired she felt, much too tired to make another meal today. She put some bacon into a skillet, broke four eggs into the same skillet, and sliced two more slices of bread. The children watched with big eyes.

"Melissa," Rachel said, "you'd better try to eat something too. We don't want you getting sick on us. Will you try?"

Melissa shook her head no, but then she got up and moved to the table. "I'll try," she said, sounding as if she had a heavy cold.

In less than ten minutes Rachel filled three plates with steaming food and dropped into a chair beside Melissa. "How about introducing us to your children?" she asked.

Melissa looked surprised, then apologized. "Yes. This is Joel. He's six years old. And my little girl is Evie. She's three. Joel and Evie, these people are Dr. and Mrs. Dorland."

Now Tom shook his head. "No, if you're going to be with us awhile, I'm Tom and this is Rachel." He patted Rachel on the top of her red head. "Rachel loves children. Did anyone tell you that?"

No one said much until the plates emptied. Rachel, fearing she'd fall asleep if she stayed in the chair, got up and started taking dishes from the table.

Tom sat in the chair she'd vacated. "Now can we hear what happened?" he asked Melissa. "Or would you rather put the little ones to bed first—if we can find a place for them to sleep." He smiled kindly to let Melissa know they'd find a place somehow or other.

Rachel brought out the same blankets the Barer children had used when they stayed with them. "I'm afraid we don't have beds for you," she said in an embarrassed voice.

"Maybe Melissa could sleep on the settle," Tom suggested, "and the children beside it."

"Yes," Rachel said smiling, "but I think the floor's softer than the settle. Say! Why don't we put them on the floor in the sewing room. Then they won't have to get up until they feel like it."

They soon had snug little pallets on the sewing room floor and the children were tucked in. The three adults went back to the kitchen where Rachel managed to perk a pot of coffee.

"All right," Tom said, "let's hear it. What happened at your house tonight, Melissa?"

The edges of her eyes reddened again, and she seemed unable to answer. Then she pulled back her shoulders, cleared her throat, and began talking. "Homer didn't go to work this morning," she said with effort. "When he got up he got a gun and told us he was going to shoot all of us."

twelve

"Why ever would he do that?" Rachel interrupted to ask.

"Shh," Tom whispered. "Let her tell it her way."

"He sat with the gun pointed at me all morning. The children didn't move a muscle either. They know what a gun is. Homer cursed me and told the children how wicked I am, and how in the Bible they stoned women like me. Thank God they didn't understand what he meant. After awhile he acted sleepy. Finally he closed his eyes and I grabbed at the gun. He woke up and beat all three of us on the heads and backs with the gun handle, then waved the thing in all of our faces and told us that at ten o'clock tonight he'd shoot us. Me, then Joel, and last of all Evie. No one said a single word to him. The children didn't even cry until they got here.

"He ranted and raved for an hour, telling Joel and Evie what a terrible woman I am, and also that with a mother like me they can't be any good either. Finally he started yelling for someone to say something, but no one did. After awhile he started nodding again. I motioned for the children to be quiet and I was too. Then his head dropped onto his chest.

"I waited a few more minutes, then grabbed the fireplace poker and hit him good. On the back of his head. I think I knocked him unconscious. I grabbed a few clothes, the gun, and we ran out of the house to here." She sighed as if she'd just shoved the weight of the world onto someone else's shoulders and took a long drink of coffee.

"Well," Tom said. "Does he know where you'd go?"

She shook her head. "I hope not. As far as I know he's never heard of you people."

Tom looked at her as if she were a much-loved child. "You know I'm a doctor, don't you? I have to go make sure he's all right."

Melissa jumped from her chair. "No! Please don't go over there. If you do, he'll know where we are."

"I don't think so. I'll just stop by."

"Please."

"I'll stay with you," Rachel said. "We'll just wait here."

Tom took his medical bag and hurried down the street, slipping and sliding in the icy snow.

"Is your husband really as nice as he seems?" Melissa asked.

Rachel nodded. "Yes, even nicer. How many men would put up with all the people we have here? We already had nine children to care for. Now it'll be eleven!" When Rachel blinked her eyes, she had to force them open again. She tried to smile to encourage Melissa. "But I'll have you to help me now. That'll be so nice."

"I hope we get to stay," Melissa said. "I hope—I hope—" She tried again and managed to bite out, "I hope I killed him. I really do, Rachel."

Melissa didn't say much more, and despite the shock of Melissa's statement, Rachel nodded off several times. If she could just drop into her soft feather bed, she'd be happier than she'd ever been in her life.

As they waited for Tom to come back, Gabriel awakened and had to be nursed, then Jesse woke, so Rachel fed him too.

"Those babies look exactly alike," Melissa said. "How do you ever tell them apart?"

Rachel rubbed an index finger down Jesse's velvet-soft cheek. He smiled, still nursing, and reached for her finger.

"When they were first born, Tom and I couldn't tell them apart either," she said. "But they don't look alike anymore to us. I don't know why and I don't know if I could explain how we tell. Maybe Jesse's face is a little rounder. For sure he wears a smile more. But it's not just the smile. We really can tell now. I think Gabriel's eyes may be a bit bluer. There's a definite difference. We long ago took off the ribbons."

The front door opened and Tom came in, his face weary. "Your husband's all right," he said, "but he's pretty mad. We'll have to swear Max and Wilma to secrecy since they'll know you're here."

"How did you get in without telling him how you knew he'd been hurt?" Melissa asked.

Tom grinned. "Oh, I just told him I'm a doctor, made up a name, and asked if that person lived there. He told me his woman waited until he was asleep and attacked him."

"He's right," Melissa agreed. "That's exactly what I did. But he left out the important parts of the story."

"Could we please go to bed?" Rachel asked. "I'm really tired."

The next morning Rachel found Melissa in the kitchen. She'd already made a fire in the cook stove and had coffee perking. Rachel felt too tired to even instruct her, so on her own Melissa made a huge pot of oatmeal, biscuits, and gravy. All the children thought the change a wonderful treat.

"Well, it looks like a school or something," Melissa said, looking over the many children after Tom left. "What do we do now?"

"I bathe all the Barer children plus my own. What about yours?"

Melissa thought a moment and shook her head. "They don't have accidents anymore and I don't bathe them every day, so why don't I do the dishes while you do the bathing?"

As Rachel bathed the children, starting with the youngest, she began to think what a help Melissa would be. But she also had to realize what a huge family they had now—and what a responsibility. Just the food they ate was a major consideration.

But when afternoon came, and Melissa insisted on scrubbing the clothes, Rachel didn't think of anything except thankfulness. She fell into bed beside Tommy and slept for over an hour until Gabriel yelled for food and woke up the entire tribe. And it all started over again.

Rachel set a batch of bread to rise, then walked into the back yard to see the snow. The pure white snow with the sun shining in the blue sky and the nap she'd just had made her feel she lived in a wonderful world. She stood drinking it all in.

"You know where my wife is?"

The rough voice jerked Rachel's mind back to reality. She hadn't heard the man approaching. She'd never seen the man before, but she had a good idea who he was. What should she say? *God, could You forgive me if I told this horrible man a lie to protect his family?*

"I have no idea who your wife is, nor you for that matter." Rachel turned her back to the man and brushed the snow from a low-hanging limb.

"My wife's name is Melissa Witlow."

Rachel ignored him, pushing the snow from another branch.

He allowed her to push the snow around for about two minutes, the longest two minutes Rachel had ever endured. "You got my wife in your house?"

"Why would I have your wife in my house?" She turned her back to him again, then whirled back to face him. "I don't think I like you very much. For all I know you don't even have a wife. Please leave right now, Mr. Witlow—or whoever you are."

He stood staring into her eyes. "I think you got 'er. If you do, you're in big trouble, coming 'tween a man and his woman." He turned and marched around the house.

Rachel dashed into the back door, fearing he might go in the front. "Get into the bedroom, quick," she whispered to Melissa. "He's here."

The man banged on the door a few times but left when no one answered.

"We'd better leave," Melissa said. "He knows we're here now and he'll kill us when he finds us."

Rachel shook her head. "He's not sure. He wouldn't have left if he knew for sure. This is the safest place for you."

When Tom came home, he wasn't pleased to learn the unstable man had been there. "Makes me feel like not going to work," he said, "but I have to. You keep the door locked and don't open it unless you know who's there."

ða

Rachel got a good night's sleep that night and felt better than she had for several days. Melissa seemed to have taken over the breakfast preparation. This time she made pancakes and dried apples with maple syrup.

Before Rachel had the children bathed, Mrs. Gump rapped on the door. "I'm so happy to see you have free time now," she said. "Do you have the clothes ready?"

Rachel hadn't even thought of the clothes. How could she have so completely forgotten? Maybe she didn't love the Lord as she should! She'd better make it up to Him— and fast. "I'm sorry," she said. "Can you give me a few more days?"

"Yes, I can do that. I'll be back day after tomorrow. Goodbye, my dear."

"Why would you sew clothes for that pompous old woman?" Melissa asked.

"Melissa! She's not a pompous old woman. She's the Ladies' Aid leader. And I don't sew clothes for her. I sew them for people who need them."

"Oh. Well, you don't have time for that kind of thing. Has the woman ever noticed how many children you take care of?"

"I don't think so. What she's noticed is that she needs clothes and I have a sewing machine."

Melissa squealed with joy. "You do? You really do? Will you teach me to sew? I'll sew the clothes for the needy children."

Rachel told her she'd be glad to teach her to sew if they ever found time with all the things they had to do.

Rachel had to make bread almost every day now. She could hardly believe her big family ate five or six loaves each day. Melissa did the washing each day, and Rachel hung it in the clothesline room as they'd started calling the spare bedroom.

ﻬ

Before Rachel knew it, Sunday came. Melissa didn't want to go to church, so she offered to care for Rachel's babies. Tom shook his head. "They have to go where Rachel does. In case they get hungry."

As they walked through the church door, Rachel had a strange feeling, as if she'd forgotten something. Sitting down, they distributed the babies between them.

When Deborah Cline rushed down the aisle toward them, Rachel felt uneasy again. Then it popped into her head. She'd agreed to teach the class! Why hadn't she stayed home with Melissa? She just couldn't face those children again!

"The children are waiting for you," Deborah whispered into Rachel's ear.

Rachel cast a desperate glance at Tom who looked confused. "I distinctly remember telling you Rachel can't do that anymore," he whispered.

Deborah smiled at Rachel in a conspiratorial way. "I know, but I had a feeling you were managing Rachel, so we had a talk. She's glad to do it, aren't you, Rachel?"

Rachel didn't know whether to agree or run out the church door. Finally she got up, laid Gabriel in the pew beside Tom, and began the long and tortuous walk back to the classroom.

The lesson went somewhat better than the last one had, if only because she didn't say anything that could get her into trouble. The children weren't any better behaved than last week, though. Some picked on the others; the others cried. Hardly anyone listened as Rachel tried to teach them about Jesus' love for them.

Rachel broke into tears as she and Tom walked home. "I can't do it, Tom. By Sunday I'm so worn out I need to rest and soak up whatever spiritual food is being served. Maybe some time I can do it, but not right now." *Inasmuch as you have done it for the least of these you've done it for Me.*

She said the words out loud, then turned frightened eyes on Tom. "Every time I decide I can't do something for someone those words come to me. Maybe I'm supposed to do it, Tom." With that thought, a new burst of tears ran down her cheeks.

Tom, carrying Tommy and Jesse, moved to Rachel and kissed her salty cheek. "Why do you think you have to do everything, Rachel? Do you think you'll be lost eternally if you don't? Don't you know salvation is a free gift from God—because He loves you so terribly much? You can't buy God's love any more than these babies can buy our love. He loves you because you're His child, Rachel, as you love these three because they're our children."

Rachel thought as they walked along. "I'm not trying to buy His love, Tom," she finally blubbered. "I want to do things for Him because He loves me so much. And I love Him more than I can say."

"He knows that, love. But He wants you to take good care of yourself—because He loves you far more than you love Him."

Rachel switched Gabriel onto her other arm. These babies were getting heavy. They needed some way to get to church besides walking.

Her thoughts went back to the day Deborah Cline had come. Rachel had asked Tom to tell the woman she couldn't teach the class. After Tom had told the woman, she'd come to Rachel. And Rachel had been able to say no. Tears bubbled up behind her eyes again, but she swallowed hard and closed her eyes tightly.

"I can't tell people no when they ask me to do something for the Lord," she wailed.

Tom smiled. "I had a hunch that was the case. I've noticed our house is overflowing with your yeses." He peered ahead. "I do believe I see our house waiting impatiently for us. My arms are tired. I'll bet yours are too."

By the time they climbed the porch steps and stepped into the front room, Rachel wondered how she'd clung to Gabriel so long.

"You two took a long time," Melissa said, stepping into the room from the kitchen. "I have dinner all ready." She looked around and out the front window. "Is it going to be just us?"

Rachel sighed. "Yes. Isn't it wonderful?"

Melissa pulled a roast from the oven with potatoes, onions, and carrots around it. *Mmmmm*. It looked good. They gathered their little ones around the table, asked the blessing, and began filling plates.

Before Rachel had taken a bite, someone pounded on the door. Tom wiped his mouth with a napkin and moved to the door. He opened it only enough to speak to the person outside.

"I want my wife out here! Right now!" a rough voice said.

Tom stepped outside and closed the door behind him.

"Well, so much for eavesdropping," Melissa said. "I suppose we might as well go with him and save you two a lot of trouble."

When Joel and Evie heard their mother say that, they both started crying.

"No, Mama," Joel sobbed. "No. I'm not going."

"No," Evie cried. "Don't go."

Rachel put a hand on each of the children's shoulders, but she looked at Melissa. "Wait and see what Tom says. He usually knows what's best. Let's go ahead and eat this delicious food." She forced herself to put one bite after another into her mouth, hoping to convince the children everything was under control.

Eventually Tom came back in and eased the door shut. "I think I convinced him to stay away from here," he said, buttering his slice of bread. "I told him he's not welcome on my place when he acts unstable, and that we're responsible for nine children here every day. I didn't mention that we also had another two staying here now, and when he asked how many of them were his, I named our babies, the Barer children, and the Johnsons. I told him that we feed them three meals a day and often their parents too." He grinned. "Everything I said was the truth, but I guess I didn't give him a chance to ask pointed questions."

Rachel sighed. She had so much faith in Tom and his morals that she was sure anything he did would be right. But then a childish saying popped into her mind. "Tom, have you ever heard this? 'Half-truth—whole lie.'"

He grinned. "I've heard that. Have you heard this one? 'Anything is legal, moral, and necessary if it helps a man protect his own.'"

"No. Where'd you hear that?"

He laughed. "I just made it up. Right now. I also told the man I'd have the police on him if he comes around anymore when I'm not here. I told him he acted so strange he scared you really bad."

Melissa laughed but didn't say anything. It all sounded good to Rachel. Hopefully, the man would abide by Tom's homemade rules.

That night after Rachel and Melissa put the children to bed, the three adults sat at the kitchen table with mugs of coffee. A knock at the door interrupted their quiet talk.

"It's him," Melissa said. "If it is, I'm going with him. Otherwise, he'll never leave you alone."

"No, you aren't going with him," Tom said, pushing his chair away from the table. "I saw how frightened those two children are of that man."

He hurried to the door, and a moment later he came back to the kitchen with the four doctors following him. "You already know my wife," he said, "and this is a friend of ours who's visiting. Would you like to sit at the table with coffee again?"

The men looked at Melissa. "Maybe we could talk in the living room," the tall gray-haired one said.

Melissa jumped up. "I'm simply beat. If you'll excuse me, I'm off to bed."

When she disappeared up the stairs, the doctors moved to the table, and Rachel served them coffee.

"Well," Tom said easily, "I presume this visit means you've come to some kind of decision."

"Yes," the blond mustached one said. "We decided we'd compare records. We all believe you're sincere in your mistaken beliefs. Therefore we take it for granted that when you see your error you'll change your methods of treatment."

Tom's smile reached nearly from one ear to the other. "That's wonderful," he said, "and I certainly will." He looked from one man to another until he'd met each one's gaze. "And I presume if it should turn out the other way, you'll all do the same."

Rachel saw surprise on at least one face. Soon each wore his professional mask again. "Of course," the gray-haired doctor said. "That goes without saying. Doesn't it, gentlemen?"

After a moment of silence, one by one the doctors assured Tom that was definitely the case.

Suddenly, Rachel realized she shouldn't be there when this happened. "Are you planning to compare records tonight?" she asked. When they told her yes, she hurried to bed, said her prayers, and dropped in, realizing she didn't feel quite as totally drained as she had so many nights in the recent past. She fell asleep and didn't waken until Gabe called—every two hours.

When morning came, she reached for Tom and found his place empty. Coming wide awake, she looked around the room. Hadn't he come to bed at all? Maybe something terrible had happened!

thirteen

She found him in the kitchen where he'd started oatmeal and coffee. "What happened?" she demanded. "Why are you up so early?"

His grin and bounce almost relieved her anxiety.

"Well, we went over the records. Then we went over them again." He looked as if he was about to soar to the kitchen ceiling. "Rachel, those records told the story so plainly no one could misunderstand them. We had several almost identical cases. The doctors who are the most ardent bleeders and purgers lost every one of those patients; the ones who take a more moderate view saved some of their patients, simply by stopping treatment. And my patients convalesced better than any of theirs. They were impressed, Rachel. I could tell they were."

Rachel felt a huge weight roll from her shoulders. "So that's the end of your problems?" she asked.

"I don't see how it could be otherwise." He grabbed her, kissed her, and twirled her around. "I see lots of blue skies ahead for us, love, if you can just learn that you don't have to do everything for everyone."

Rachel squirmed from his arms. "I've learned my lesson too, Doctor. Don't you worry about me anymore."

"What's going on out here?" Melissa said, laughing from the doorway. "Do I have to be here every second to keep you two in line?"

In a little while Max Barer and Wilma Johnson arrived with their six children. As they hurried off to work down the board sidewalk, Rachel noticed them laughing together. When

Rachel prepared to bathe the children she found the Barer young ones didn't need a bath.

"Who gave you a bath and washed your clothes?" she asked Lester, the oldest.

"Miz Johnson helped. She gave the little 'uns baths but said I'm 'bout old enough to do it myself."

Well! Rachel wondered how that had come about. She didn't have much time to think about it because her busy day began and pushed her before it as she did the things that had to be done.

About ten o'clock a buggy stopped in front of the house, and Mrs. Gump alighted, then helped another woman down. The other woman didn't look quite steady on her feet.

"Rachel, this is Mrs. Cynthia Buchanan," Mrs. Gump said after helping the woman into the house. "She's sick and has no place to go. Her husband died two years ago and she has no children or other relatives. I told her you'd be glad to take her into your large family. Why with all the children you have, you won't even know she's here."

I'll know she's here, Lord. Tell me what Your wish is. Please, Lord, tell me. Rachel didn't hear anything and she couldn't stall forever. What could she say? If she took in this woman she'd be taking in Jesus, wouldn't she? *You have to ask Tom, Rachel.* She was sure that was her answer. *Thank You, Lord. Of course, I do.*

"Have you noticed how full our house is, Mrs. Gump? There isn't always room for one more. Really there isn't. I can't do anything until I talk to Tom." She glanced at the clock on the mantle. "He'll be here in a little over half an hour so you'll have to give me a couple of hours to decide whether we can."

"She doesn't want me," Mrs. Buchanan whimpered to Mrs. Gump. "Come on, let's go."

"I didn't say that, Mrs. Buchanan," Rachel said kindly.

"I'd enjoy having another adult around, I really would, but we have to come up with a place for you to sleep, especially since you're sick. I'm wondering, too, how you'd get along with eleven children yelling and crying all the time. It's hard, even for those of us who aren't sick."

"Eleven children? I couldn't stand the uproar. Come on, Mrs. Gump, let's go."

But Mrs. Gump wasn't interested in going. "I can't find any other place for her," she said quietly to Rachel. "I have no idea what will happen if you refuse to take her in." Her lips set in a thin straight line. "We'll sit on chairs on the porch until you decide."

Rachel grabbed Mrs. Gump's arm. "No, you won't. Not in this weather. You can sit here in the front room and watch the children." She giggled. "Sometimes they're entertaining."

"What a fool!" Melissa said as they hurried to make dinner and put it on the table. "Everyone in this town runs right over you."

Rachel smiled tremulously. "It's because I love the Lord so much," she said. "I want more than anything in the world to please Him."

"You aren't doing it for the Lord," Melissa said. "You're doing it for these pushy people who won't lift a hand themselves to help anyone."

Melissa put the split pea soup on the table, and Rachel put on the roast meat sandwiches she'd made. Two entire loaves of bread had gone into those sandwiches.

Rachel heard Tom's cheery voice in the front room as he greeted the women. After they told him they were waiting for Rachel, he came out to the kitchen. Rachel saw a big question in his eyes as he kissed her hello. "Later," she whispered.

After Tom asked God to bless the food and also the partakers, the three adults filled fourteen dishes with soup and dispensed fourteen half-sandwiches. "Now I'm going to take something to the ladies," Rachel said. "I'm sure they can smell the food and they may be hungry."

She returned a moment later with empty hands. "They acted as if I'd given them a feast," she said. Then she quietly told Tom what they wanted.

"I thought I had you convinced that you can't take care of everyone in the entire world," he said. "There have to be people in this town who aren't loaded down as you are."

Melissa kept the children happy and their bowls filled with soup while Rachel shook her head and said, "You didn't hear her, Tom. She said no one in town would take the woman in and she didn't know what would happen to her if we don't take care of her."

"That speaks pretty terribly of the town and its people, don't you think?" Melissa inserted.

Tom looked almost grim. "I think it only speaks of the woman who said it."

"Mrs. Buchanan is sick, Tom," Rachel said. "The woman seems to be real sick."

That got Tom's attention. "What's wrong with her?" he asked with interest.

Rachel laughed. "I don't know, Tom. I'm not the doctor in this family."

Tom grinned. "Think she'd talk to me?"

"She'd have to if she lived here. Shall we try it for a few days, Tom? Maybe we could help her."

"And what about you? I doubt it will help you much. Melissa might have something to say about it too. I notice both of you are busy from morning until bedtime with the work you already have."

"I'll be happy to help if you want to take her in," Melissa said to Rachel. "I've never seen anyone who loved people and God as much as you do."

Rachel looked at Tom. He smiled. "Let's try it but only for a few days," he said. "Now I have to get back to my rounds."

"Thank you, Tom. You'll never be sorry. That's what my mother told me lots of times. That I'd never be sorry for helping anyone. But that I'd almost for sure be sorry for not helping."

Rachel took a plate of sandwiches to the ladies, then a bowl of soup. Both ladies took seconds, Mrs. Gump a whole sandwich and a large bowl of soup, and Mrs. Buchanan a half bowl of soup.

Rachel sat down beside Mrs. Buchanan. "We've decided to try it for a few days," she said. "Do you still feel you can't handle all the children? They'll be here for a long, long time."

Mrs. Buchanan smiled wanly. "I don't seem to have a choice. I can't take care of myself right now."

Rachel began to feel kindly to Mrs. Buchanan. "We'll get you well before you know it," she said. "I'll cook nourishing food for you, and my husband's a doctor. He'll be caring for your medical needs."

The woman almost jumped off her chair, but she soon settled back weakly. "Oh no, he won't," she said with more strength than she'd shown before. "I'm through with doctors. I'll go home and die alone before I ever let another doctor touch me. Doctors only make people worse."

Whoa! Rachel didn't know how to reply to the woman's outburst. She couldn't promise her that Tom would leave her alone. "He won't force himself on you," she assured Mrs. Buchanan. "You'll still be in charge of your own life. But we'll all be very interested in your well-being and will be asking how you are. Will you put up with that?"

The woman relaxed somewhat. "Yes, I'll be thankful for your interest." She smiled. "And your food. Your food was so good. Better than anything I've had for years."

"Good," Rachel said. "Maybe you just need some good food. You look awfully frail."

Mrs. Gump harumphed twice, then interrupted. "I need to be getting back now. No telling what's come up while I was gone. I'll bring in your things, Mrs. Buchanan. I borrowed a buggy to bring her over here," she told Rachel. "I don't feel comfortable driving a horse, but I suppose I can get it back to its owner."

Rachel met Melissa's eyes. "Where can we put her?" she asked.

Mrs. Gump brought a box of clothes and set them inside the door. "I have to get back now and see what I have to straighten out next," she said. "Goodbye. Goodbye, Mrs. Buchanan." Rachel and Melissa watched Mrs. Gump gingerly climb into the buggy and pick up the reins, looking terrified.

"Could you sit here a little longer while we try to figure a comfortable place to put you?" Rachel asked.

"Don't bother about me," Mrs. Buchanan said. "I can sleep anywhere."

But Rachel wanted to find some place where the sick woman wouldn't be bothered by the children any more than necessary. They had three bedrooms upstairs. The largest was the room she, Tom, and the babies used; the next room contained Rachel's sewing supplies, including many for the church, but Melissa and her children slept on mats on the floor. They hung the laundry in the third bedroom, and the lines were full all the time now.

"I just mentally went through the house and didn't find a place for her," Rachel told Melissa. "If we didn't have so many children we could put a bed in the front room for her, but we do. We definitely do."

"I know the perfect room," Melissa said, "but it's already

full."

"Where? What room?"

"The dining room. We've never eaten in there once since I've been here, but it's full of furniture."

The dining room. It would be perfect. Almost. The noise from the children would be bad there, but otherwise the room would be private. "What could we do with the furniture?"

Melissa looked sad for a moment, then her face set. "Would you like for me to take my little ones and go somewhere else?"

Rachel shook her head vigorously. "Don't ever mention that again, Melissa Witlow. I couldn't begin to handle this place without you now." She giggled. "Besides I don't think we'd dare put Mrs. Buchanan on the floor of the sewing room."

"Thank you," Melissa said humbly. "Could we put the dining room furniture on the porch for now? Or would the rain and snow wreck it?"

"We might as well wait until Tom comes home," Rachel decided. "We don't have a bed anyway. Let's go put Mrs. Buchanan on Tom's and my bed."

So they did that, then hurried into the work that had fallen behind in the course of the day, the washing, the breadmaking, the dishwashing.

Rachel decided to hang the clothes outside as the sun shone brightly. They might not dry, but they never dried quickly in the clothes-hanging room. As she hung the clothes on the line, Homer Witlow appeared beside her, scaring the breath out of her. "I'm not goin' to hurt you," he said before she could say a word. "I been watching your place. Why all the goin' ons if you ain't got my woman?"

Rachel drew a deep breath and determined not to let the man know he'd frightened her so badly. "It isn't any of your business what we do at our house," she said. "Why are you snooping around anyway?"

"'Cause I want my woman back."

"We took in an old sick woman today so I can feed her right and my husband can help her get well. Just in case you think you have a right to know her name, she's Cynthia Buchanan. Right now I have her in my bed, but when Tom gets home we'll try to figure out a place for her to sleep. We really don't have room for any more people in our house, so you may as well look somewhere else for your kin."

"I'm goin' inside and have me a look around. If you don't have my woman I'll leave and not come back." He turned around and started toward the house.

Rachel grabbed him by the back of the shirt and jerked hard. As he fell back she jumped out of his way. When he landed, he grunted as though the breath were knocked from him. Rachel leaned over him, her eyes meeting his bloodshot ones. "Don't you ever mention breaking into my house again, you tramp," she yelled. "I have three of my own babies in there as well as six other small children and a sick woman. Don't you even think about going in there with all those precious lives. I'll make you sorry you were born."

He nodded his head while struggling for breath. Rachel took one last look at the man, then ran for the house as fast as she could go.

"He's out there," she puffed to Melissa. "Don't go out or even to a window. I hurt him but it won't last long."

Right then Tom came whistling up the sidewalk. When he opened the door, Rachel threw herself into his arms. "He's out there, Tom. Get him. Go get him!"

Tom thrust her away from him so he could look into her eyes. "Who's out there, love?"

"Homer Witlow. I pushed him down, Tom, and he's probably mad."

Tom walked around the house, then came back in. "I didn't see anyone out there, but part of your washing is gone. Or didn't you hang it all outside?"

"I did. That awful man took it, Tom. I know he did."

"Come out with me and see what he took. I have an idea I already know."

Rachel went out and soon discovered he'd taken his family's clothes. Now he knew for sure they were here!

fourteen

"Tom, he knows they're here. What do we do now?"

He reached for her hand. "I don't know, love. Let's pray about it right now." They bowed their heads in the back yard and each asked the Lord to protect Melissa, the children, and themselves from the wicked man. When they went inside, they didn't mention the new development to Melissa. Tom just quietly told her to be sure to stay inside the house and also to keep the children inside.

After eating a good meal, Tom and Rachel moved the dining room furniture to the storage shed behind the house. "It'll be all right there until Mrs. Buchanan gets well," Tom said. Then he hurried down to the General Mercantile to buy a bed.

Rachel and Melissa bustled around the dining room, giving it a good cleaning before putting Mrs. Buchanan into it. Rachel had told the sick woman where they were putting her, and she'd been pleased. "I'll like being closer to everybody," she said.

Tom came back in a dray from the store. He and the delivery boy put the narrow bed in the room and set it up. They set a dresser with a mirror against the other wall.

"Have I ever told you what a good husband you are?" Rachel asked while Tom helped her put the sheets and blankets on the soft feather-bed he'd bought.

Tom grinned as he straightened the last blanket, then pulled Rachel to him. "I'm not good," he whispered in her ear. "I'm just eager to get this patient in my hands so I can persecute her."

Rachel knew better. But she also knew he couldn't wait to talk to the woman to see what had been done to her by doctors to make her distrust them so much.

When they had everything ready, Tom helped Mrs. Buchanan down the stairs and into her bed. Rachel tucked her in. "Do you need anything? Are you hungry? Or cold?" Rachel asked.

The woman shook her head. "I'm perfect," she said. "Now you just go on about your business and I'll be fine."

Tom pulled up one of the three dining room chairs they'd left in the room. "Do you feel like a little visit?" he asked, straddling the chair, his arms lying along the back. Rachel pulled another chair to the edge of the bed and smiled at the wan woman.

"We'd like to know a little more about your sickness," Tom said. "Do you know what's wrong with you?"

"No. But after what that doctor did to me, he should know everything."

"How are you sick, Mrs. Buchanan? Where do you hurt?"

Her translucent hand moved to her throat. "I had a sore throat to begin with. And a headache and I just felt bad all over."

Tom nodded. "And what did the doctor do for you?"

"The idiot gave me poison that made me throw up everything I ever ate in my whole life. That made me sicker. Naturally. Then he started taking my blood."

"Do you know how much blood he took?"

She shook her gray head. "No, but it looked like a quart in the jar he used."

Tom nodded. "It could have been. How did you feel after that?"

"It made me so weak I could barely move my body around." She squinted a moment as if thinking. "I was already weak from the vomiting."

"Did he do anything more?"

"Yes. After several days he took some more blood, not as much that time."

Tom nodded again. "Were you getting better by then?"

She shook her head. "I couldn't walk one step alone. About three days later he brought me some stuff that was supposed to make me have diarrhea. He said I still had too much vitality and he had to get rid of some of it. That would have killed me, I could feel it in my bones, so I flat out refused and told that doctor I never wanted to see him or any other doctor again."

Tom took her hand and rubbed the back of it. "I think you'll like my treatment a little better," he said with a mischievous smile.

She jerked her hand away and started to sit up but let herself back down. Then her eyes met his, weak but still fiery. "I don't think so, Doctor, because you aren't going to treat me. I meant what I told your wife. I'm never going to let another doctor touch me. I may be old but I can tell when I get worse instead of better."

Tom chuckled quietly. "Won't you even listen to my suggested treatment? I'll tell you a little secret, Mrs. Buchanan. I'm in trouble with the other doctors in town because I agree with you. I neither bleed nor purge my patients and I'm having great success. Makes those doctors mad too."

The sick woman looked surprised, then brightened. "Well, I could listen to what you want to say. That don't mean I'll let you touch me."

"I don't want to touch you. I want you to rest and eat as much of my wife's chicken soup and other good things as you can hold—as often as you can get it."

Mrs. Buchanan smiled all over her face. "I'll follow those instructions exactly, Doctor."

Tom got up and patted her shoulder. "Good. Now I want

you to get to sleep and sleep as long as you can. Good night."

Rachel echoed Tom's good night and followed him from the room. "Well, Tom," Rachel said as they undressed for bed, "finally I believe your treatment is better than the bleeding and purging. I really do."

Tom leaned over and deposited a kiss on her lips. "Took an old woman to convince you, though, didn't it?"

ॐ

Morning came too soon, though Rachel could tell she wasn't quite so exhausted since Melissa came. Suddenly she realized she'd miss Melissa a lot if the woman left.

Mrs. Gump came early, and she didn't take gracefully Rachel's excuse of forgetting about the sewing.

"Don't worry, Mrs. Gump," Melissa said. "I'm going to learn to sew and I'll work hard on your clothes."

Mrs. Gump didn't look as pleased as Rachel thought she should. "That's all well and good," she said, "but why don't you just watch the children while Rachel makes the clothes? She's an expert, you know."

That afternoon Rachel spent the time the children napped teaching Melissa how to use the sewing machine. Then she cut out some diapers, as they were the simplest of clothes, and helped Melissa hem them.

Rachel's father appeared as they worked on the sewing. "What's new with you?" he asked Rachel after she kissed and hugged him. "Has that old hawk brought you more clothes to make yet?"

Rachel and Melissa laughed. "As a matter of fact, that's what we're working on right now," Rachel said.

"Why don't you just throw the stuff out the front door and be done with it?" he asked, his eyes merry.

Then the children awakened, and Nate played with them while the women attacked their daily afternoon tasks, the washing and the breadmaking.

Rachel kept looking over her shoulder as she hung the

clothes on the line outside in the clear but freezing day. What would she do if that awful man came back? This time she couldn't hope to make him believe his family wasn't here. She hurried and finished with no sight of him.

Immediately after Tom came home, a group of eight doctors called on him. "Let's sit in the front room," Tom invited, since there were too many to crowd into the kitchen.

"I'll get right to the point," the tall gray-haired man said. "Our entire medical community met last night and we were severely reprimanded for exchanging medical records."

"Excuse me," Tom said, "but I don't believe the entire medical community was there. I wasn't even notified of the meeting, let alone invited to attend."

"Uh—yes. But to get on with my story. The other doctors said comparing one person against a group would give the one a distinct advantage every time. They voted to continue treating according to established medical knowledge, forgetting all this experimental stuff, leaving that to the scientists." He looked around at the other doctors who, except for Tom, were all smiling and nodding.

Dr. Couperous leaned forward. "So we're here to inform you that in Oregon City, Oregon, people can expect the best medical care, the proved and approved method of treatment."

Tom looked far from happy. "I'm disappointed in you men. We saw together how purging and bleeding weakens a person. I can't force you folks to advance with the times in your practice, but I certainly won't be a party to this giant step backwards."

The blond doctor cleared his throat. "I'm afraid we haven't made ourselves clear, Doctor Dorland. The entire medical community has agreed that if you want to practice in our city, you must give up these unfounded ideas you've been espousing."

Tom started to get up but sat back down. "I suppose you

want an answer to your ultimatum. Here it is. I took an oath to do my best to help people stay healthy and to regain their health when they lose it." He shook his head from side to side in a determined way. "I'll never subject my patients to procedures that make them worse rather than better. I guess that's it, gentlemen."

The men moved in their seats nervously until Tom spoke again. "Oh yes, I plan to practice in Oregon City for many years." He chuckled. "At least the people here will have a choice, won't they?"

After a little more shuffling in their seats, the doctors got to their feet. "Thank you for allowing us to use your home for a meeting place," the blond man said.

"Anytime," Tom said. "I hope there are no hard feelings. I guess not everyone can think alike."

"Yes," the older, gray-haired man said. "I guess we'll have to meet again to decide what's next."

"You going to have another meeting of the medical community?" Tom asked.

"Yes, I think so."

"Well, don't forget to invite me."

As the doctors walked down the sidewalk, Max Barer and Wilma Johnson hurried toward the house, seeming to have much to say to each other. Max's children never seemed eager to see him, but tonight they willingly went home, some hanging onto Wilma's hand.

"Whew!" Melissa said, "let's get supper on the table. Hey, we didn't tell Max that his children hadn't had supper."

Rachel pulled the huge pot of stew from the back of the stove and began filling bowls. "Don't worry," she told Melissa, "the children will tell him."

Tom led his family into Mrs. Buchanan's room for prayer. He thanked God for the food and asked Him to heal the sick woman.

"Thank you, Doctor," Mrs. Buchanan said. "I never had anyone pray for me before."

After filling bowls with stew and buttering bread for the children, Rachel fixed Mrs. Buchanan a tray and took it in to her. When she returned for the tray, she discovered the woman had eaten everything she'd taken to her.

Later that evening, Tom and Rachel told Melissa her husband had taken her and her children's clothes from the line. Melissa insisted she had to go back to him to reduce the danger to Tom and Rachel and their children. "No telling what Homer will do to get even," she said.

"No," Tom said. "You aren't going back to him. Not tonight or ever. You don't know our God, do you, Melissa? He's very powerful so we're going to ask Him to protect us all. God will put a barrier around us that no one can penetrate—so don't give a thought to leaving."

Tom and Rachel knelt near Melissa, who sat on the settle. "Dear Father God," Tom began, "we thank You for loving us so much You gave Your one and only Son to die for our sins so we can live with You. We eagerly look forward to the day You will return to claim Your own so we can be with You for ever and ever. Now, Lord, You know everything, so You realize we're in some danger here. We pray for Your protection for everyone in our home so we won't have to be fearful or hide. In the meantime we'll do our best to follow You in word, thought, and deed. We thank You and praise You for answering our special prayer in Jesus' name. Amen."

Rachel prayed a similar prayer, ending by thanking God for loving her so much and telling Him that she loved Him with all her heart and mind and strength and soul. When she opened her eyes to get up, she noticed Melissa wore a half-smile.

"Could you tell me exactly how your God is going to keep

Homer from hurting us?"

Tom grinned. "He always hears and answers our prayers, Melissa. How'll He keep Homer away? I haven't the slightest idea. Maybe he'll change Homer's heart, if Homer will only let him. But even if Homer hardens his heart against God, God will still answer in His own way."

Mrs. Buchanan grew stronger and felt better each day. She told Tom that she thoroughly approved of his method of treatment. "Just letting me get well," she said. Tom and Rachel both continued to pray for her to heal and for protection for Melissa as well as themselves.

Tom didn't hear anything from the doctors, but Rachel heard from Mrs. Gump. "I think it's time you did a little more than sew a few clothes for children," she said one morning. "We need someone once a month to clean the church. Can I write you down for that, since you have someone to leave the children with?"

"Mrs. Gump," Rachel said, trying to sound firm, "we're still caring for eleven small children. That's far too many for one person to handle, even for one day. I know—for I used to do it alone."

"I believe it's expected of us to sacrifice a little for God, don't you?"

Inasmuch as you have done it for the least of these, you've done it for Me. Rachel sighed. She'd forgotten how it felt to have any energy. Now she felt thankful to be able to stagger into her bed at night. "Let me talk to my husband, Mrs. Gump. He works hard and it isn't fair to ask him to do more than he is already."

"I've been hearing your husband is soon going to have nothing but time. Maybe I should just go ahead and put his name on it."

Rachel's breath left her at the cruel words. "What do you mean by that?" she rasped.

"I'm sure you know, my dear. Isn't he about to quit practicing medicine?"

Tom just smiled when Rachel told him what the nasty woman had said. "Don't worry a minute about her," he said. "But don't you remember our talk about not killing yourself off with everyone else's responsibilities? God doesn't expect or want you to do that, Rachel."

fifteen

Rachel smiled. "Are you sure, Tom? Didn't Jesus say that a true friend will lay down his life for his friends? I could probably clean the church one week a month without killing myself."

Tom shook his head. "You have enough to do, love. You tell her no. I mean it this time. Why do you have to do so much, Rachel? Are you trying to be good enough for heaven?"

"Maybe. I'm not sure. I just know that the verse, inasmuch as you do this for one of the least, you do it for Me, pops into my mind every time someone asks me to do something. I don't know, Tom, but I love Him so much, I just want to keep doing things for Him."

"I think you're trying to be good enough for Him, Rachel, and you can never do it. You will surely kill yourself trying, because you can never ever buy your way into heaven. Jesus paid your way. You can never buy His love. That's why He died for you. Because He loved you so much. His love's free, Rachel, and heaven's free too. It's His love gift to you."

"Don't you think He wants me to do things for Him?"

Tom gathered her into His arms. "He loves You, Rachel, and therefore He loves to do things for you—and loves for you to do things for Him. But this has gotten way out of hand. You know that, don't you? You're doing the work of two women. Melissa is doing the work of two women too. Have you ever wondered why she does it? Well, she loves you a lot. Because of her strong love for you, I'm hoping we'll be able to teach her to love our Lord one of these days too. Think how it was for you before Melissa came. You went around so tired you could hardly see. God wants you to take care of yourself too, you know."

Rachel thought about what Tom had said. He was right, of course.

A couple of days later Mrs. Gump came by. Rachel shuddered when Melissa let her in. The woman would no doubt have plenty to say when she told her Tom said she had enough to do.

But Mrs. Gump had forgotten all about cleaning the church. As soon as she got inside the door, she grabbed Melissa and hugged her, patting her shoulder at the same time. "I'm so sorry, my dear," she said into Melissa's ear. "If there's anything the church can do for you, just let us know. At a time like this a woman needs all the support she can get."

Melissa met Rachel's eyes over Mrs. Gump's shoulder, raised her eyebrows, and shrugged.

What could be wrong? All eleven of the children were in the house, playing and well. "What is it, Mrs. Gump?" Rachel asked. "What's happened?"

Mrs. Gump looked shocked. "What? You mean you don't know!" She grabbed Melissa again. "Oh, my dear. I didn't want to be the one bearing bad news. Sit down, ladies, and I'll tell you."

Rachel and Melissa sat together on the settle. Melissa reached for Rachel's hand. Mrs. Gump sat on a chair facing them and looked from one to another. Rachel thought she saw eager anticipation in her eyes.

"You must be brave, Melissa," the woman finally said. "A tree fell on your husband this morning and crushed him to death."

Melissa's eyes grew round as she stared at Mrs. Gump. It seemed as if she stopped breathing, but eventually she drew in a long, shuddery breath. "I don't believe it," she whispered. She sat ramrod stiff, no expression on her face at all.

Rachel didn't say a word. Neither did Mrs. Gump. *Please, God, get this woman out of here. Melissa needs to be alone right now. I think she's in shock.*

Almost immediately Mrs. Gump gathered herself together and got up. "I'd best go," she said, "and let you two get used to the dreadful news. Be sure to call on us if you need anything." She moved out the door with no more conversation.

"Rachel—" Melissa began and stopped, unable to go on. She opened her mouth again, stopped again.

"I know it's a shock, Melissa." Rachel asked. "But maybe you'll feel better if you can talk about it."

Melissa nodded her head wildly up and down. She didn't look broken-hearted, Rachel realized; instead she wore a strange expression, as if she had something important to say. Rachel decided to wait patiently, holding her hand, until Melissa could talk.

Finally Melissa jumped up and jerked Rachel to her feet. "Did you hear?" She pointed toward the door Mrs. Gump had long since disappeared through.

"I heard," Rachel said. She tried to take Melissa into her arms but Melissa backed away. Again, Melissa pointed to the front door, waving her arm up and down. Then she pointed straight up. "God—" she began and stopped. "He—He—He answered our prayers!"

Rachel dropped back onto the settle. Melissa looked happy! Excited! In fact, she seemed overjoyed. Melissa's eyes met hers, looking as if she'd just learned something too good to be true. "What did you say?" Rachel whispered.

"I said God's real! He answered our prayers. He loves us, Rachel! He takes care of us." She fell onto the settle beside Rachel and hugged her close. "I think I love Him!"

Rachel shook her head to clear it. "Melissa!" she said firmly. "Are you all right? Do you remember what Mrs. Gump told us?"

Melissa jumped up and whirled around. "Of course, I do. We don't have to hide and be afraid anymore. Homer won't ever bother us again." She fell to her knees, folded her hands in front of her. "Thank You, God. I love You and will do only what You want me to forever."

Rachel didn't know how to relate to Melissa's reaction to her husband's death. Before she could think what to say, Tom rushed through the door. He looked from Rachel to Melissa and back to Rachel. "You haven't heard," he said in a low flat voice.

Rachel hurried to him. "We have heard," she whispered. "Melissa's taking it sort of strangely."

"Yes, we've heard," Melissa repeated. "Isn't it wonderful?"

Tom's eyes opened in surprise. "I'd never call a death wonderful."

Melissa looked surprised at Tom's comment. She shook her head. "No, no, not Homer's death, but God's wonderful answer to your prayer. Remember you asked God to keep Homer away from us so we wouldn't have to hide and fear for our lives anymore? Well, He answered, Tom. He answered!"

Tom looked dazed. "That wasn't what I meant when I prayed, Melissa."

She looked as if she were explaining something simple to a child. "I know you didn't, but you also said God answers in His own way and it's always the best way. You tell me, how else could He have made Homer leave us alone?"

Rachel couldn't keep quiet any longer. "Do you think this is God's answer to our prayers, Tom?"

Finally Tom grinned. "I'm not sure, but you two better

not mention this to anyone else. I wouldn't want people thinking we prayed for a man to die. That would really finish us off in this community."

"He was your husband," Rachel said. "I guess you'll have to be responsible for the funeral and whatever has to be done."

A determined look crossed Melissa's face. "Next you'll be telling me that I have to act sad, when I just learned to love God and believe in Him." She looked from Tom to Rachel, squared her shoulders, and went on. "I'm not sorry Homer's dead. If I were, I'd be spitting on God's answer to prayer."

Tom smiled at Melissa. "Will you settle for not rejoicing when people are around? I'm not asking you to be a hypocrite. I know the man hurt you and your children. But he was your husband, and once you must have seen something in him to love. Because of that, I'm asking you to be respectful of the dead. Now—let's get something to eat. Then I'll help you go make the arrangements."

"What arrangements? Can't we just have them bring him here? And have the service tomorrow and then bury him?" A stricken look crossed her face. "Oh, Rachel, I can go home now. I can go home. I can go home now." She burst into tears. "But I don't want to go home."

"You don't have to go home until you want to," Rachel said.

"And you can have the service here," Tom added. "I think you're in shock right now. I suspect that pretty soon it'll sink in that Homer's gone and you'll feel differently. In the meantime, you need to be here, with people who care about you."

Melissa's face brightened. "Thanks. I would like to have the service here. I've never had any friends like you two before. And now I have God too. I don't think you two understand what happened. God just proved Himself real to me. He loves us, protects us, and answers our prayers. How can I not be happy?"

❧

Late that afternoon Mrs. Gump came again. "I came to offer you the church for the service," she told Melissa, "even though neither you nor Mr. Witlow attended there."

Rachel could see Melissa trying to fit on her face a look of respectful grief, as Tom had asked. "Thank you," she said, her face serious. "But we're having it here."

"Oh. I thought Rachel would have the funeral dinner here as you're her friend, but not the service too."

Melissa didn't miss a beat. "We will have a funeral dinner here, Mrs. Gump, but under the circumstances I don't think we'll invite the church. We'll just do it quietly ourselves."

"Are you sure? No one has ever done this before."

Melissa nodded. "I know, but people are usually church attenders and—well, this time it's just different. You tell everyone thank you but this will be best."

After the insulted woman left, Melissa asked if she had done the wrong thing.

"Not if that's how you want it," Rachel said. "It'll save us a mountain of work. But I'll bet a lot of people won't come to the funeral if they don't get a free dinner out of it."

That evening Tom brought a newspaper home folded open. He tossed it onto the table and pointed at it. "Better take a look at this," he said. "The doctors are more upset with me than I thought."

Rachel picked up the paper and saw a large notice covering the entire page. The letters "TOM DORLAND" appeared in very large print, followed by several lines of smaller print. "Dr. Tom Dorland is not practicing medicine according to American Medical Association knowledge and guidelines.

We urge the community not to use his services as his methods have been determined to be ineffective as well as dangerous. The Medical Association cannot be responsible for his actions." The words were followed by the signatures of every other doctor in Oregon City.

When Rachel raised her eyes she found Tom's pained gaze on her. "What do we do now?" she asked.

He shrugged. "I don't know. I have a wonderful practice right now. Probably better than any of theirs." He pecked a finger on the newspaper as he said "theirs." "I have more patients because people have learned by word of mouth that I treat my patients differently and also that my methods work. But I have no idea what this will do to my practice. Let's put it out of our minds until after the funeral tomorrow."

Three families came to the funeral, and Tom invited them to stay for dinner. Rachel enjoyed the dinner better than any of the funeral meals she'd attended. Maybe because fewer people made less work. Maybe because Melissa wasn't morose and enjoyed the meal too. Melissa's children, Joel and Evie, weren't upset either, thanks to Melissa's attitude and also her careful preparing of the children for the service.

Mrs. Buchanan came out from her bedroom and ate with the group. She said she felt perfectly well enough to help, but Rachel told her there was nothing more to do.

"Shall I take Evie and Joel and go home now?" Melissa asked after everything was cleaned up.

Tom smiled at her. "Only if you want to."

Melissa shook her head. "I'd like to stay here a few more days if you don't mind." She looked at Rachel and giggled. "Or forever."

"Stay," Tom said. "As long as you want."

The next day when Tom came home for dinner he looked gloomy. "I lost two patients this morning," he said.

"Oh, Tom," Rachel said running to him. "I didn't know

you had any critical patients right now."

Tom burst out laughing. "I guess that puts things into perspective," he said, looking happier. "I lost the patients to another doctor. They both explained they hadn't realized how it really is, and that all the other doctors could hardly be wrong and one right."

"I guess that's the way it sounds," Rachel said. "But I still believe in you."

They put the children to the table and fed them. Then Tom went back to his rounds.

About mid-afternoon Mrs. Gump arrived in a buggy. She'd come in a buggy before only the time she'd brought Mrs. Buchanan, so Rachel hurried out to see what she'd brought this time.

The woman shoved several huge boxes from the buggy. "Help me take these inside, will you?"

sixteen

Rachel grabbed one side of the box and together they managed to get it into the front room, then the next two, and finally the last.

"I'd like a schedule this time," Mrs. Gump said. "Why don't you figure out how long it'll take you to do each box? Do it right now so we can both plan on it."

Material! More material. Rachel thought of her huge family, including Mrs. Buchanan who felt much better but still needed lots of care. "I should never have helped you unload all those boxes," she said. "My family is as big as it's ever been, plus I have Mrs. Buchanan here now. I still have the four Barer children, the two Johnson young ones, my own three babies, and the three Witlows. Melissa and I both work from the time we get up until we go to bed at night caring for the children, cooking, cleaning, baking, washing clothes. Doesn't that sound like we're doing enough?"

Mrs. Gump tsk-tsk-tsked. "We really must care for others beyond our own families, my dear. Remember the verse, inasmuch as you have done it for the least of these, you've done it for Me."

As soon as Rachel heard the verse her heart sank. "I'm sorry," she said. "Could I have a few days to figure out a schedule? Right now we're in a state of reorganization."

Mrs. Gump looked more than pleased. "Of course, dear. Take three or four."

When Tom came home later, he found Rachel in tears. She told him about Mrs. Gump's visit. "I know God wants me to do it," she said, "but He's expecting too much of me. I simply can't do more."

"God isn't expecting too much of you," he said. "You and Mrs. Gump are, but He isn't. He knows what He made you from. Clay—dust, Rachel. And you aren't going to do it this time. You've let that woman run your life until you haven't a minute to yourself, until you're so exhausted you can't even function." He went into the front room and looked at the boxes, then took Rachel into his arms again. "Why did you ever let her unload all that stuff on you anyway?" he asked with a grin.

Rachel sniffed one last long sniff, and pushed back her hair. "Because I thought the Lord wanted me to."

"Well, you just forget that. You're doing more for Him than anyone I've ever known. And you simply must convince yourself that you can't pay Him for His love. He loves you because you're His child, not because of anything you can ever do. Remember, Rachel. Just as you love Tommy, Gabriel, and Jesse."

Rachel felt a peace she hadn't felt for some time. *Thank You, God, for Your beautiful peace. And for wonderful Tom. Bless him, Lord.* Rachel sat down and played the piano for a full half hour, the longest she remembered playing since the twins had been born. She felt a warm blessing.

❧

The next day Tom came home for dinner wearing a long, bleak face.

"Whatever's wrong?" Rachel asked, a dark feeling growing in the pit of her stomach.

He tried to smile. It turned into more of a wince. "I keep losing more patients," he said. "I've already seen everyone today. I have only about a half-dozen left. They've all said the same thing. They hadn't realized I'm so far from the rest in my practicing." He managed a genuine smile and took her hand. "Six patients won't go far in supporting our large family."

Rachel nodded. "I'm glad we've been saving money. But that won't last forever with the crowd living here. What's going to happen, Tom? Will the people forget and come back to you? Or will they see that your treatment really is better?"

"I'm afraid the other doctors won't let the people forget I'm the strange one, going against medical practices. I met two of them on the street today. They sort of apologized but said they would put more notices in the paper if necessary. They aren't telling the people that I follow the more progressive doctors in Europe. Or that the American doctors are way out of date."

"What can we do then?"

Tom leaned against the sideboard. "How would you like to move?"

"Where? Tom! We can't move. Look at all the people who depend on us."

He chuckled out loud. "I thought that was one of the reasons we should move. Give you a new start where you listen to the Lord, not everyone who wants to push his responsibilities onto you. You're God's misplaced angel, Rachel, who thinks she has to do everything that gets done. Anywhere. Everywhere. Anyway, we're about to lose the Barer and Johnson children, don't you think?"

Rachel wondered what he meant, then remembered the growing friendship between Max Barer and Wilma Johnson. If those two ended up married, Wilma would quit working and care for their own children. Rachel nodded. "Yes. I think you're right."

"And Mrs. Buchanan is well. She's talking about going back to her own house. What's stopping us, Rachel? Where should we go?"

"Do we have to, Tom? We have this nice home and friends here."

"I can't practice medicine according to someone else's beliefs, Rachel. One day they'll all realize they're wrong, but in the meantime I can't abuse the Hippocratic oath. Would you want me to farm or cut timber, even though I know nothing about it and love medicine?"

No. She could never ask him to give up medicine. Their original plan for her to help him in his work flashed across her mind. She'd loved helping him, but it hadn't worked out. Somehow she'd gotten so involved with helping everyone else she hadn't had time for Tom. "Where, Tom? Where would we go?"

"The world's open," he said. "Pick a place. Any place."

Martha Lawford! She'd missed Martha so badly and longed to see her. Would Tom want to go that far? It seemed Walla Walla Valley in Washington was halfway back to Missouri, but she knew it wasn't.

"How far would you want to go?" she asked, her voice quivering with eagerness.

"As far as you feel up to traveling with the young ones."

Suddenly Rachel remembered the horrors of the Trail. How could she handle all that again? "I was thinking about Walla Walla Valley," she said, feeling much less excited than she had a few minutes earlier. "You remember Martha Lawford? I loved her so much and still miss her."

"Of course, I remember Martha. What a faith that girl has. The Walla Walla Valley sounds great to me. Are you sure she's still there?"

"Where could she go? Remember she had a wagon with nothing to pull it? I could hardly bear to leave her there alone, but I prayed hard for God to send someone to help her. And He assured me He had. Let's go back to Walla Walla, Tom. Dan and Julia Barlow are there too. I think I'm getting excited."

Tom thought Walla Walla would be a good place to settle too, but he said they should stay in Oregon City for awhile—until all his patients either left him or got well.

Melissa burst into tears when she heard they were leaving the area. "How can you just go off and leave me?" she asked at supper that night.

Tom laughed as he shoved a bite of food into Tommy's open mouth. "Who said you have to stay?" he asked. "Walla Walla's just as nice as here, though not as civilized. Why don't you come along?"

"Yes!" Melissa yelled, so loudly that Gabriel jumped and burst into tears. Rachel turned him over her shoulder and talked softly into his ear.

"Yes," Melissa repeated not quite so loud. "When can we start? What do we need for the trip? I can sell my house and buy whatever we need."

"I'd love to go too," Mrs. Buchanan said. "I know the trip would be hard on me, but what am I going to do for a doctor? I'll never let those other doctors treat me again. I have plenty of money to pay my way."

Melissa broke into wild laughter. "You're leaving to get away from all the people who depend on you—and now you're taking them with you?"

"No," Rachel said. "You're wrong. We're not leaving to get away from our responsibilities. Tom wants to get me away from people who take advantage of me." Her eyes darted from Melissa's face to Mrs. Buchanan's. "And you two never do that."

Tom and Rachel talked later and decided Mrs. Buchanan should go with them if she really wanted to. "If we take her, I'll at least have one patient," Tom told Rachel, chuckling.

ঽৈ

Melissa begged Tom not to take the church's material back.

After she finally caught on to the sewing machine, she used every spare minute she could find or make to sew one of the large boxes of material into clothes. When Mrs. Gump came to check, she must have been surprised, but she didn't flicker one eyelash.

"I'll check again next week," she said. "I knew you two could do it if you'd just give a few minutes to the job each day. Doesn't it make you feel good to know you're doing something for someone else?"

Melissa and Rachel laughed until they collapsed onto the settle after the pompous woman left. "As if she had any idea how it feels to help others until you drop," Melissa said. "Let's get busy on the next box."

Within a week, Max Barer and Wilma Johnson told Rachel they were getting married, and Wilma would be taking over the children. "I never did like to work anyway," she told Rachel. "And neither of us will be lonely anymore."

"She may not be lonely," Melissa said when they left, "but if she thinks taking care of his four and her two won't be work, she has a lot to learn."

A week later the couple shyly told Rachel they'd been married that day and wouldn't be bringing the children anymore. It seemed that Rachel and Melissa had hardly anything to do after that. Caring for their own children, with Mrs. Buchanan's help, left them plenty of time to finish the huge boxes of material. They turned them into clothes in record time.

Even Mrs. Gump showed surprise and pleasure. "I'll get a buggy and haul them away," she said. "I'll bring you more material when I come after the clothes. You're an angel, Rachel."

"Don't bring any more, Mrs. Gump," Rachel said. "We're leaving the area and definitely won't have time before we leave. If you bring more, you'll have to take it back with you." *There, God. Did that sound firm enough?*

"Oh, you can't leave," Mrs. Gump said. "There's no one in the whole city who does as much as you. And no one has a house big enough for special dinners, nor the time to prepare them."

Somehow Rachel wasn't surprised. But she let it go. "We have to leave," she said. "The doctors have driven all Tom's patients away so we have no choice."

The next afternoon Deborah Cline, the Sunday School superintendent, came rushing into the house. "I heard you're leaving," she puffed. "You simply can't, Rachel. We can't get along without you. No one else will teach that class."

Rachel took a deep breath. "I guess the children will have to stay with their parents then, because we're leaving."

≈

One day Tom announced that his last patient had recovered. "Let's sell the house and buy some oxen and wagons." In a few days word got around that the Dorland house was for sale and one of the other doctors bought it, paying Tom's price without hesitation. He told Tom they could live in it as long as they needed while they prepared for their trip. Melissa sold her house too. And so did Mrs. Buchanan.

A few days later a tall gray-haired man knocked on the door. "Heard you's goin' to Walla Walla," he said.

Rachel nodded, wondering which of their belongings the man wanted to buy. "Yes, in a week or so."

The man shifted his weight to the other foot. "Well, we was just wonderin'. We've had our three grandchildren for a couple years now. Their pa and ma left them while they went to find a place to live. They got a donation claim now and a right nice cabin so we wondered if you'd be willin' to take the young ones to their folks. We'd be glad to pay whatever it'll cost you."

Rachel drew in her breath. Did she have a big mark on

her forehead telling everyone to dump their children on her? Was this God's will? Maybe they should do this since they were going anyway. Then she thought about the trip. At best it would be stressful with her three babies and Mrs. Buchanan. Even with Melissa's help the trip would be hard. *Show me what You want me to do, Father. Help me to know. Please, Lord.*

Immediately she felt peace. And a voice spoke to her heart. *This is your trip, Rachel. Make it a good one. You can give someone a cup of cold water in My Name when you get to Walla Walla.*

She met the old man's eyes. "I'm sorry, but we have five children to care for already, three of them babies. We simply can't handle any more."

The man stiffened just a little. "This here's the only way we got to get the younguns to their ma and pa. It ain't like we ain't willing to pay. We'll pay whatever you-uns want."

Rachel shook her head. "It's not the money, sir. We just physically can't do it. The trip will be harsh enough anyway. We can't do it, but I'm sure you'll find a way to get them there."

Tom, having heard the conversation, came to the door and stood beside Rachel. "Hello," he said, extending his hand. "I'm Tom Dorland and this is my wife, Rachel. I have an idea. Why don't you get yourself set up and travel along with us? Walla Walla's a long way from Oregon City. You might like to live nearer your kin anyway, and this would be a good way to make the move."

"We're too old to make the trip, but I'll pay you to take 'em. I'll pay you good."

Rachel shook her head again. "We can't take your children, sir, not for all the gold in the West. If you decide to make the trip with us, just let us know within the next week. Goodbye now."

When she closed the door, Tom grabbed her in a giant hug. "Well, my sweet little misplaced angel," he said, "I think you finally have it figured out. That was masterful."

❧

Tom bought three wagons for them and two for Melissa, oxen to pull them all, and hired men to handle the oxen. "I'll be too busy helping you with the children to handle oxen," he told Rachel with an excited grin. "We'll probably carry these young ones all the way."

Nate Butler, Rachel's father, decided to go with them. He bought only one wagon, since he didn't have many things now that Alma was gone.

"Is this going to kill oxen and people as the Trail did?" Rachel asked. "I can't go through that again."

"No. It's early spring. We have plenty of time so we won't have to hurry. We'll be there long before winter no matter what. No, love, it won't be anything like the Trail."

Rachel fixed up one wagon with beds for them and the babies, making it as comfortable as possible for the babies who would have to live in it. For herself, she couldn't handle the thought of riding and making the oxen pull her extra weight.

She smiled, remembering how she'd begun the Oregon Trail—sitting in her wagon like a queen. By noon the first day, every inch of her anatomy had ached so badly she could barely move. It hadn't taken long for Martha to convince her it would be easier on her as well as the oxen for her to walk. They'd walked the two thousand miles from Independence, Missouri to Walla Walla, Washington together.

Rachel packed her sewing machine in one of the wagons, but Tom insisted she sell the piano. She felt bad to leave it, but she didn't make a big fuss as she had when she and her father had left Illinois. She'd been young, spoiled, and self-centered then. And she hadn't realized how awful it would be for the animals pulling the wagons. She'd much rather sell the piano than to hurt the oxen.

They fixed the last wagon into a little home for Mrs. Buchanan, who insisted she could walk to Walla Walla as well as any of them—if they'd just keep that good food coming her way.

Melissa fixed her wagons to her liking, hauling as many of her belongings as Tom thought she could.

ஒ

"Well, we're nearly ready," Tom said one day. "Is everyone excited?"

Everyone was, especially Joel and Evie, Melissa's children.

"The trip should take about a month. If it takes two, who cares? We're just going to take it slowly and enjoy the trip. Let's gather around now and ask the Lord's blessing."

"Our Father, God," Tom began. "We thank You for going with us on the trip ahead. But we ask more than Your presence. Guide our every step, Lord. Bless us with Your wisdom, patience, and love. Give us an abundance of strength and health. Help our trip to be pleasant and may we grow closer to each other and You during the days ahead.

"And stay with us when we get there, Father. Help us to know and do Your will in our pleasure and our work. Help us to love our neighbor as ourselves and be willing to do all we can to ease his load. But help us to discern Your will from man's. And bless my work, Father. Help me never to compromise my duty to You and to man.

"Thank You again, Lord. We offer our prayer in Jesus' name and thank You for hearing and answering. Amen."

When he finished, Rachel walked into his arms. "Before you know it, you'll be with your good friend, Martha Lawford," he said. "And Lord willing Walla Walla will be our home from now on. We'll do all we can for God in our

new home, but we won't become slaves to anyone, right?"
His eyes twinkled. "Not even to the American Medical Association."

A Letter To Our Readers

Dear Reader:

In order that we might better contribute to your reading enjoyment, we would appreciate your taking a few minutes to respond to the following questions. When completed, please return to the following:

Rebecca Germany, Editor
Heartsong Presents
P.O. Box 719
Uhrichsville, Ohio 44683

1. Did you enjoy reading *Misplaced Angel*?
   ❏ Very much. I would like to see more books
      by this author!
   ❏ Moderately
      I would have enjoyed it more if _____

   _____

2. Are you a member of *Heartsong Presents*? Yes   No
   If no, where did you purchase this book? _____

   _____

3. What influenced your decision to purchase this
   book? (Check those that apply.)

   ❏ Cover   ❏ Back cover copy

   ❏ Title   ❏ Friends

   ❏ Publicity   ❏ Other _____

4. On a scale from 1 (poor) to 10 (superior), please rate
   the following elements.

   ___Heroine   ___Plot

   ___Hero   ___Inspirational theme

   ___Setting   ___Secondary characters

5. What settings would you like to see covered in
   Heartsong Presents books?

   _____

   _____

6. What are some inspirational themes you would like
   to see treated in future books?_____

   _____

   _____

7. Would you be interested in reading other *Heartsong
   Presents* titles?   ❏ Yes   ❏ No

8. Please check your age range:
   ❏ Under 18   ❏ 18-24   ❏ 25-34
   ❏ 35-45   ❏ 46-55   ❏ Over 55

9. How many hours per week do you read? _____

Name _____

Occupation _____

Address _____

City _____ State _____ Zip _____

VeraLee Wiggins

THE FORERUNNERS

_**Heartbreak Trail**—While Rachel Butler gains in strength physically traversing the legendary Oregon Trail, her heart struggles to keep pace. Reverend James Richards is the handsomest man on the wagon train, but the young physician, Tom Dorland, has a quiet appeal Rachel can't deny. HP76 $2.95

_**Martha My Own**—Martha's journey on the Oregon Trail ends in the Washington Territory where hard times continue to plague her. Rescued more than once by the heroic and faithful Abram Noble, she and Abram resort to a marriage in name only so she can survive. HP83 $2.95

_**Abram My Love**—Abe Noble's love for Martha Lawford knows no bounds. Yet their tacit agreement—a marriage of convenience, one in name only—denies such feelings. Together as they battle the forces of nature in the early years of Washington State, will Abram and Martha realize the forces of love? HP92 $2.95

_**Misplaced Angel**—Rachel Dorland lives by this Scripture: In as much as ye have done it unto one of the least of these my brethren, ye have done it unto me. Soon Rachel finds herself caring for seven children, plus her own. Rachel is so tired she can barely think, but how can this misplaced angel turn away her Lord? HP128 $2.95

Hearts♥ng

HISTORICAL ROMANCE IS CHEAPER BY THE DOZEN!

Buy any assortment of twelve *Heartsong Presents* titles and save 25% off of the already discounted price of $2.95 each!

Any 12 *Heartsong Presents* titles for only $26.95 *

*plus $1.00 shipping and handling per order and sales tax where applicable.

HEARTSONG PRESENTS TITLES AVAILABLE NOW:

___HP 1 TORCH FOR TRINITY, *Colleen L. Reece* *
___HP 2 WILDFLOWER HARVEST, *Colleen L. Reece* *
___HP 7 CANDLESHINE, *Colleen L. Reece*
___HP 8 DESERT ROSE, *Colleen L. Reece*
___HP 11 RIVER OF FIRE, *Jacquelyn Cook* *
___HP 12 COTTONWOOD DREAMS, *Norene Morris* *
___HP 15 WHISPERS ON THE WIND, *Maryn Langer*
___HP 16 SILENCE IN THE SAGE, *Colleen L. Reece*
___HP 19 A PLACE TO BELONG, *Janelle Jamison* *
___HP 20 SHORES OF PROMISE, *Kate Blackwell* *
___HP 23 GONE WEST, *Kathleen Karr*
___HP 24 WHISPERS IN THE WILDERNESS, *Colleen L. Reece* *
___HP 27 BEYOND THE SEARCHING RIVER, *Jacquelyn Cook*
___HP 28 DAKOTA DAWN, *Lauraine Snelling*
___HP 31 DREAM SPINNER, *Sally Laity*
___HP 32 THE PROMISED LAND, *Kathleen Karr*
___HP 35 WHEN COMES THE DAWN, *Brenda Bancroft*
___HP 36 THE SURE PROMISE, *JoAnn A. Grote*
___HP 39 RAINBOW HARVEST, *Norene Morris*
___HP 40 PERFECT LOVE, *Janelle Jamison*
___HP 43 VEILED JOY, *Colleen L. Reece*
___HP 44 DAKOTA DREAM, *Lauraine Snelling*
___HP 47 TENDER JOURNEYS, *Janelle Jamison*
___HP 48 SHORES OF DELIVERANCE, *Kate Blackwell*
___HP 51 THE UNFOLDING HEART, *JoAnn A. Grote*
___HP 52 TAPESTRY OF TAMAR, *Colleen L. Reece*
___HP 55 TREASURE OF THE HEART, *JoAnn A. Grote*
___HP 56 A LIGHT IN THE WINDOW, *Janelle Jamison*
___HP 59 EYES OF THE HEART, *Maryn Langer*
___HP 60 MORE THAN CONQUERORS, *Kay Cornelius*
___HP 63 THE WILLING HEART, *Janelle Jamison*
___HP 64 CROWS'-NESTS AND MIRRORS, *Colleen L. Reece*
___HP 67 DAKOTA DUSK, *Lauraine Snelling*
___HP 68 RIVERS RUSHING TO THE SEA, *Jacquelyn Cook*
___HP 71 DESTINY'S ROAD, *Janelle Jamison*

*Temporarily out of stock.

(If ordering from this page, please remember to include it with the order form.)

·········Presents·········

__HP 72 SONG OF CAPTIVITY, *Linda Herring*
__HP 75 MUSIC IN THE MOUNTAINS, *Colleen L. Reece*
__HP 76 HEARTBREAK TRAIL, *VeraLee Wiggins*
__HP 79 AN UNWILLING WARRIOR, *Andrea Shaar*
__HP 80 PROPER INTENTIONS, *Dianne L. Christner*
__HP 83 MARTHA MY OWN, *VeraLee Wiggins*
__HP 84 HEART'S DESIRE, *Paige Winship Dooly*
__HP 87 SIGN OF THE BOW, *Kay Cornelius*
__HP 88 BEYOND TODAY, *Janelle Jamison*
__HP 91 SIGN OF THE EAGLE, *Kay Cornelius*
__HP 92 ABRAM MY LOVE, *VeraLee Wiggins*
__HP 95 SIGN OF THE DOVE, *Kay Cornelius*
__HP 96 FLOWER OF SEATTLE, *Colleen L. Reece*
__HP 99 ANOTHER TIME...ANOTHER PLACE, *Bonnie L. Crank*
__HP100 RIVER OF PEACE, *Janelle Burnham*
__HP103 LOVE'S SHINING HOPE, *JoAnn A. Grote*
__HP104 HAVEN OF PEACE, *Carol Mason Parker*
__HP107 PIONEER LEGACY, *Norene Morris*
__HP108 LOFTY AMBITIONS, *Diane L. Christner*
__HP111 A KINGDOM DIVIDED, *Tracie J. Peterson*
__HP112 CAPTIVES OF THE CANYON, *Colleen L. Reece*
__HP115 SISTERS IN THE SUN, *Shirley Rhode*
__HP116 THE HEART'S CALLING, *Tracie J. Peterson*
__HP119 BECKONING STREAMS, *Janelle Burnham*
__HP120 AN HONEST LOVE, *JoAnn A. Grote*
__HP123 THE HEART HAS ITS REASONS, *Birdie L. Etchison*
__HP124 HIS NAME ON HER HEART, *Mary LaPietra*
__HP125 FOREVER YOURS, *Tracie J. Peterson*
__HP126 MISPLACED ANGEL, *VeraLee Wiggins*   *Temporarily out of stock.

Great Inspirational Romance at a Great Price!

Heartsong Presents books are inspirational romances in contemporary and historical settings, designed to give you an enjoyable, spirit-lifting reading experience. You can choose from 128 wonderfully written titles from some of today's best authors like Colleen L. Reece, Brenda Bancroft, Janelle Jamison, and many others.

When ordering quantities less than twelve, above titles are $2.95 each.

Heartsong Presents
Love Stories Are Rated G!

That's for godly, gratifying, and of course, great! If you love a thrilling love story, but don't appreciate the sordidness of popular paperback romances, **Heartsong Presents** is for you. In fact, **Heartsong Presents** is the *only inspirational romance book club*, the only one featuring love stories where Christian faith is the primary ingredient in a marriage relationship.

Sign up today to receive your first set of four, never before published Christian romances. Send no money now; you will receive a bill with the first shipment. You may cancel at any time without obligation, and if you aren't completely satisfied with any selection, you may return the books for an immediate refund!

Imagine. . .four new romances every month—two historical, two contemporary—with men and women like you who long to meet the one God has chosen as the love of their lives. . .all for the low price of $9.97 postpaid.

To join, simply complete the coupon below and mail to the address provided. **Heartsong Presents** romances are rated G for another reason: They'll arrive *Godspeed!*